The Flower H
Cottage

De-ann Black

Toffee Apple Publishing

Other books in the Cottages, Cakes & Crafts book series are:

Book 1 - The Flower Hunter's Cottage.
Book 2 - The Sewing Bee by the Sea.
Book 3 - The Beemaster's Cottage.
Book 4 - The Chocolatier's Cottage
Book 5 - The Bookshop by the Seaside

Published by Toffee Apple Publishing 2015

The Flower Hunter's Cottage

ISBN: 9781520782355

Toffee Apple Publishing

Also by De-ann Black (Romance, Action/Thrillers & Children's books). See her Amazon Author page or website for further details about her books, screenplays, illustrations, art and fabric designs.
www.De-annBlack.com

Romance:

The Sewing Shop
Heather Park
The Tea Shop by the Sea
The Bookshop by the Seaside
The Sewing Bee
The Quilting Bee
Snow Bells Wedding
Snow Bells Christmas
Summer Sewing Bee
The Chocolatier's Cottage
Christmas Cake Chateau
The Beemaster's Cottage
The Sewing Bee By The Sea
The Flower Hunter's Cottage
The Christmas Knitting Bee
The Sewing Bee & Afternoon Tea
The Vintage Sewing & Knitting Bee
Shed In The City
The Bakery By The Seaside
Champagne Chic Lemonade Money
The Christmas Chocolatier
The Christmas Tea Shop & Bakery
The Vintage Tea Dress Shop In Summer
Oops! I'm The Paparazzi
The Bitch-Proof Suit

Action/Thrillers:

Love Him Forever.
Someone Worse.
Electric Shadows.
The Strife Of Riley.
Shadows Of Murder.

Children's books:

Faeriefied.
Secondhand Spooks.
Poison-Wynd.
Wormhole Wynd.
Science Fashion.
School For Aliens.

Colouring books:

Summer Garden. Spring Garden. Autumn Garden. Sea Dream. Festive Christmas. Christmas Garden. Flower Bee. Wild Garden. Faerie Garden Spring. Flower Hunter. Stargazer Space. Bee Garden.

Embroidery books:

Floral Nature Embroidery Designs
Scottish Garden Embroidery Designs

Contents

CHAPTER ONE

Cupid's Dart

The flower hunter's cottage was two shades darker than the snow–covered Scottish landscape that surrounded it on three sides. The front of the cottage faced the wild, grey sea. Years of harsh winds and bitter cold rain had worn away the edges of the coastline, polished the slate grey stones that led from the cottage garden down to the shore and buffeted the trees to a windswept angle.

Everything leaned against the harshness of the terrain. The flat expanse of grassland faded into the hills and distant towns whose roads were so far away that not a sound was heard from any car. The grass was hidden under a glistening quilt of unending January snow that tipped the edges of the coast before falling off the cliffs into the sea.

Even the clouds, in varying hues of grey, blew at an angle across the afternoon sky, out to the sea and islands far beyond.

Only the little cottage stood its ground, strong and steady. Built to last. And it had, for more than a hundred years.

I felt the responsibility weigh down on me as I drove towards the cottage. The list of rules and promises were ingrained in my mind. I must not alter the cottage decor in any way. I must maintain the garden as it was, as it had always been since it was first landscaped by the original flower hunter who built the cottage and created the garden. Everything was precious.

Had I made a mistake?

I'd been determined to secure the lease on the cottage. For months I'd jumped through all the hoops of paperwork and interviews. Was I any use at gardening? Did I know my daisies from my dahlias? Did I understand the significance of the work of the early flower hunters who had gone in search of new plants and flowers, scouring the world for new species and bringing them back home safely to nurture them?

Did I?

I assured them I did understand. Flower hunters from bygone times were intrepid explorers, venturing into uncharted areas of the world — jungles, forests, mountainous regions, inhospitable places filled with danger. Their trips to India, China, America and various regions of Europe to find new species of plants were taken at a time when travelling was itself an adventure. Long journeys on ships across stormy oceans, trekking through swamps and desert terrain, often sleeping where they lay, under the stars. They helped create the gardens we enjoyed today with their abundance of flowers from all over the world.

As a botanical illustrator and gardener I certainly knew about plants. And I loved the past — vintage, heritage. During the year I would live in the cottage, I promised to ensure its proper upkeep and attend to the garden better than anyone else who had applied for the lease.

Most of those who wanted the cottage were hoping for a holiday home, a traditional cottage by the sea in a beautiful part of the Scottish Highlands. But that wasn't enough. Not for the flower hunter who was leasing out his cottage while he went off abroad for a year in search of new flora. He wanted to leave the cottage in careful hands.

The company who handled his business chose me.

The keys were to be handed to me on my arrival by the lease manager, the man I'd been dealing with since October. I'd been allowed to visit the cottage one late October day when the sea mist cast everything in soft focus and the scenery's blues, greys, browns and greens were so deep and dark it felt like the white stone cottage was the only light on the landscape.

But I had loved the sense of the place. Iain, the flower hunter, wasn't home. The lease manager gave me a tour of the property.

The two–bedroom cottage had cosy fireplaces — one in the living room and one in the larger bedroom. I knew which bedroom I'd sleep in. When I moved into the cottage I'd snuggle up in bed, under one of my handmade quilts, feeling the warmth of a fire flickering at night. Apart from my botanical work, I was a quilter. I pictured that after a long day working in the garden and painting the flowers for my illustrated book, I'd sit by the fireside in the living room and sew my quilts. Depending on the weather, I'd also sit outside on warm evenings and breathe in the scent of the flowers and the sea. Sheer bliss.

Yes, I'd fought hard to secure the lease. I'd seen the cottage from afar years ago driving by on holiday to the Highlands, and when the property popped up online I made my pitch for it. It was one of several cottages in the area, sprinkled along the stretch of coast and countryside that nature had stitched together so seamlessly it didn't even show where the edges met.

Even though the cottage was by the sea, the soil was rich and dark, not at all sandy. It owed its richness to the countryside that spilled across to the sea line. The flower hunters, four generations of men from the original family, had toiled to maintain the quality of the soil, bringing new top soil from further inland to enrich the garden around the cottage.

The old–fashioned kitchen had a large sink near the window overlooking the back garden that stretched to a hedge row marking its border. Here at the window I'd chop vegetables fresh from the soil — potatoes, carrots — and make tasty homemade lentil soups and broths while a batch of scones baked in the oven.

I planned to build myself up, heart and soul. On my own, with no one to answer to, including an ex–boyfriend who owned his own business in the city and flattened every ambition and achievement I ever had.

But I was moving on. He was in the past and the city was a long way off, both in miles and in mind. I was determined not to think about him until the heartache faded to yet another bad experience on the rocky path of life.

The vintage garden with its trees, flower beds and winding stone paths would keep me occupied. One path led to the little shed where I would use the gardening tools that were themselves antiques. I would attend to the garden from the deepest snow of early January through to the spring, summer, autumn and finally winter again.

I blinked from my thoughts when I saw a car parked outside the cottage. The lease manager was waiting for me. At mid afternoon the sky threatened to call it a day and give in to the early evening twilight, but the snow created a lightness making the cottage and all that surrounded it look ethereal.

I drove up, careful not to drive over anything precious. I'd been told to stick to the main path and so I followed in the tracks of the manager's car and parked beside him.

He stepped from the vehicle, and that's when I realised it was a different man.

'Mairead? I'm Fintry. The manager you were dealing with couldn't make it,' he said, striding towards me, tall and handsome. 'He asked if I'd give you the keys. The snow has caused delays on the roads from the city. He wouldn't have been here until after dark.'

I kept looking at his mouth, so sensual as he spoke in a deep Scottish voice. His face was as rugged as the landscape and yet bore a smooth handsomeness that was quite overwhelming.

Perhaps it was the expensive cable knit Aran jumper that made him look like he'd stepped off of a high class knitting brochure, or the moss green cords, a colour match for his eyes. The expensive cut of the cords emphasised the length and strength of his athletic legs.

He. Looked. Fit.

His hair was a shock of burnished gold. He was clean–shaven with defined cheekbones sweeping up and out to the corners of his eyes. He looked at me, waiting for a reply as he handed me the keys.

'Thank you.' I clasped them tight to avoid dropping them into the snow. I'm not a clumsy person but this man was a distraction. I assumed he lived nearby. My heart fluttered unexpectedly. I had a neighbour who was one of the most luscious men I'd ever seen.

'Is there anything you need?' He towered above me, brushing the fullness of his hair back from his untroubled forehead.

He had a pale golden tan. In this weather? How could that be? Unless he frequented a tanning salon or similar, but I didn't sense that he was the type to fuss with his looks. He didn't need to. At least I didn't think so.

Maybe it was the harsh weather? Yes, he was probably weather beaten.

I realised I was staring at him.

'Well, is there?' he said, prompting me. 'Anything before I go?'

Oh don't tempt me. To run my hands through that silky hair of his and invite him in for tea.

'Would you like a cup of tea before you go?' I pointed to my car. 'I brought fresh groceries with me.'

'No, I'm fine. I have to be going.'

He walked back to his car. His sturdy boots pressed down into the fresh snow leaving an impression as deep as the one he'd already made on me.

'Do you know how to light a fire?' he said suddenly. 'The cottage is cold. I wasn't sure if I should light one or not. I wasn't even sure if you'd make it here through the snow.'

Nothing was holding me back from getting to the cottage. Nothing. Not even a snow storm. Snow had fallen overnight and snow ploughs had cleared most of the main roads. The last few miles to the cottage had been a challenge, but knowing that a beautiful cottage was waiting for me spurred me on.

'I know how, but thanks.' I hoped I remembered. As a child, brought up by my grandparents in a bungalow with a large garden and real fire, I'd set the fire many a morning to help my gran. I'd carry the coal scuttle inside, arrange the firelighters, pieces of wood and twisted newspaper, then top it with coal. Once it caught, I'd used the brass poker to urge the coal to turn, and then put the fireguard in front of it. By that time my gran would have made our breakfast and the house would start to feel as warm as the welcome I'd always felt when I was there, living with them, after I'd lost my parents.

Fintry turned and gave me a smile before getting into his car. 'Enjoy your time at the cottage.'

'Thanks, I will.'

He drove off and I watched his car disappear along the twisting road down towards the little harbour.

Damn! I should've asked him about Iain the flower hunter. If he lived nearby he'd know him personally. Never mind, I'd no doubt see him again at the niche of local shops beside the harbour. I sensed that our paths would cross again.

The wind picked up pace and whipped through my copper brown hair. I pulled my knitted bobble hat from my jacket pocket and put it on to tame the strands that had broken loose from my ponytail. I'd started the day with a tidy hairstyle, a brush of mascara to give my blue eyes a less weary appearance, and a slick of lipstick that promised to keep my lips soft and smooth on wintry days. I'd become so pale I didn't suit blusher. Even the subtle shade I used to wear looked garish on me.

'It's all the upset and heartache,' my gran said during a recent visit home. 'It takes a lot of courage to walk away from a three year relationship, even one that's soured, and go off and start a new life, especially a temporary one. Nothing is settled in your world,

Mairead, but living by the sea will put some healthy colour back in those cheeks of yours.'

I believed it would. That and meeting a handsome man like Fintry.

I breathed in the scent of the sea and the energy from the wind swirling around me. I buttoned up my jacket. Time to unload the car.

I'd brought my stash of fabrics and sewing machine with me. My grandparents kept my other belongings, not that I owned a lot. Living with a man who insisted on having an uncluttered designer house had pared even the few things I had to the bare minimum. Finally I decided to leave him and removed myself from his minimalist home. 'You'll be back,' he shouted after me.

No, I thought. I won't ever be back with you.

Stop thinking about him. Stop it.

I breathed in the cold, fresh air again and lugged all my luggage and artwork equipment inside. The front door kept blowing shut, and I used what I supposed was a doorstop, a chunk of varnished wood, to keep it open while I carried everything inside.

Finally, I closed the door and heard the silence. The thick stone walls cut out the noise from outside. All the floors were polished wood, easy to keep tidy, and homely enough with scatter rugs. The walls were painted a warm white and the doors were dark oak. There were no frills or fuss and yet the interior gave a comfortable feeling. Wherever colour was added, on the brocade curtains on the front and back windows of the lounge, or the velour cushions on the comfy sofa and chairs, it was shades of blue, from Prussian to cerulean, soothing colours of the sea.

Two table lamps gave a cosy glow to the living room, but the cottage was cold. Before I unpacked I lit a fire in the lounge and in the bedroom.

The kitchen was just off the living room. I filled the kettle and boiled it to make tea. I planned to cook dinner after I'd unpacked. Every part of the cottage had been cleaned, and with two chests of drawers and two wardrobes I soon had my belongings tidied away.

I set my sewing machine on a study table in the living room, making sure to put a tablecloth down first so as not to mark the surface. However, the surface looked like it had seen a few scratches, and there were ink marks, as if someone had used it for years as a writing desk. The table had drawers and I opened them, expecting them to be empty, cleared of all personal belongings like everything else, and was surprised to see folders containing photographs and drawings of flowers along with data about each species. The drawings were rough, but each one was named allowing me to identify the flowers that were drawn in pencil. Only a few had any hint of colour such as the blue Cupid's dart flowers, one of my favourites.

A note was pinned to one of the folders addressed to me from the flower hunter. *Me*?

Mairead. Here is the information you need about the flowers and how to attend to things in the garden. I've included data on flowering times, and if you paint any of these I would appreciate it if you could put a copy in the folders. The lease manager said that you are working on a book of flower illustrations and designs for sewing, quilting and crafting. I'm not an artist, as you can tell from my scribbles, and I'll be happy to pay you on my return for any artwork you care to add. Many thanks.

A surge of excitement swept through me. Contribute my drawings to the flower hunter's archives? Oh yes. I'd be painting the flowers anyway for my book, creating new designs for quilting blocks and motifs. It would be easy to give Iain a copy. I loved the thought of being part of the history of the cottage.

I put the folders back, closed the drawers and went through to the kitchen to make something to eat. Something easy. I'd brought a loaf of bread, milk, tea bags and general tinned groceries with me. I opened a tin of chicken broth and heated it on the stove while I cut a wedge of cherry cake and made a pot of tea.

I set up a table beside the fire in the living room and ate dinner there. The soup and slices of crusty bread were delicious and just what I needed — like the cottage, nothing fancy, but wholesome and comforting.

As I watched the snowflakes start to flutter down outside the window I realised I was truly alone, and yet I felt totally safe. Safe in the cosy cottage on a snowy night beside the fire. It was magical.

As I cleared the dishes away and made a fresh pot of tea to finish the last pieces of my wedge of cake, I wondered if I was seeing things when I gazed out the kitchen window.

Was that a man trudging through the snow heading towards the cottage? Was that an oil lamp he was carrying?

I cupped my hands on the glass. The tall figure of a man wearing a thick winter jacket with the hood pulled up carried a lamp in one hand and...I couldn't make out what was in the other. Two lamps? One glowing in the darkness.

Should I be concerned?

There was no point in hiding and pretending I wasn't at home. He must've seen me lit up at the window.

A gloved hand gave me a friendly wave.

The doors were bolted and I intended keeping them that way until I found out exactly who he was and what he wanted at this time of night.

CHAPTER TWO

Sweet Peas

I watched the man pick his way carefully across the garden, familiar with its layout. Even when it was covered with snow he knew where the paths were and avoided walking on the flower beds.

He walked up to the kitchen window and shouted through to me. He was quite attractive from what I could see of his face peering out from the hood of his jacket. 'Sorry to disturb you, Mairead, but there's a storm warning. I brought a couple of hurricane lamps for you in case the power cuts out.' He held up the lighted lamp.

'Hurricane?' I said so loud that he heard me.

'No, no, the storm's not that fierce, just a fair blustering, but I heard you'd arrived and thought you might need these.'

His face and tone seemed friendly and my instincts didn't sense that he was dangerous.

He smiled at me. Nice smile.

'I'll leave these on the doorstep.' He put the lamps down and stood back trying to show he meant me no harm. Giving me a friendly wave, he started to walk away.

Lamps. Hurricane. Power cut. All alone in a cottage in this weather. Man trying to be neighbourly. Okay. I unlocked the kitchen door and called to him.

'Thank you.'

He turned. 'You're welcome. There should be oil in the cottage to refill the lamps. Do you know how to light them?'

Blank look.

He started back across the garden, and as he approached the kitchen door I realised he was as tall as Fintry, not as refined, but very manly.

He picked up one of the lamps and gave me brief instructions on its use.

I accepted the lamp from him and picked up the other one from the step.

'I've made a pot of tea. Would you like a cup before you go?' He was well–dressed for the weather, but he was obviously cold and goodness knows how far he'd trudged to get to the cottage.

'I wouldn't say no.' He kicked the snow from his boots and pulled the hood of his jacket down as he stepped inside the kitchen, revealing a head of dark, unruly hair. He had to be over six feet tall. I barely came up to his shoulders.

I unhooked a mug from the rack and poured the freshly brewed tea from the pot. 'What do you take in your tea?'

Hazel eyes gazed down at me. 'A splash of milk and one sugar.' He eyed the cherry cake that was minus one slice and then looked away.

'Slice of cake?' I said, cutting him a wedge before he had the chance to reply.

'Thank you. I'm Tavion. I live in one of the cottages. I heard you'd taken on this place.'

'I suppose with this being a small community everyone chats about newcomers arriving.'

'I think it's true what they say. If you want a lonely life, go live in a city. We're a wee niche but everybody knows everybody.'

I carried his tea and cake through to the living room and he sat down opposite me at the fire.

A gust of wind hit the cottage. The house didn't flinch, but I jumped at the sound of the snow storm sweeping across the coast.

'Do you live far from here?' I asked him.

'Not too far. Don't worry, I won't stay long. I'll finish my tea and cake and get back before the storm gets any worse.' He bit into the cake. 'Very tasty. Did you bake it yourself?'

'No, it's shop bought, but I'm hoping to find time to bake and enjoy living the rural life.'

His lips curved into a quirky smile. 'Finding time.' He shook his head and continued to focus on his cake. 'You're a city girl, aren't you?'

'I am, but I was brought up in my grandparents' house in a town on the outskirts of the city. They had a huge garden, and although this is all new to me, I know about gardening and how to look after myself and the cottage.'

'I didn't mean any offence,' he was quick to say. 'I just meant that...living in the city, the pace is so fast that folk have to scrabble to find time for anything.'

'No offence taken.'

He glanced at my sewing machine and my artwork case.

'I'm going to be painting flowers while I'm here, and sewing. Though I suppose you know that already.'

'Sorry. We're a bunch of gossipmongers.'

I smiled at him. 'What about you? What do you do?'

'I'm a flower grower.'

'Not a flower hunter?'

He shook his head. 'I'd like to have been, but I'm not like the men from this cottage — always heading off to various places in search of new flowers. An adventurous life, but an uncertain and unsettled one. I like my home. I guess I'm a homebody at heart. My cottage is further inland and I've got fields where I grow my flowers.'

'What happens in the winter months?'

'Despite the weather there are only a few weeks when there's heavy snow. For most of the year there's always work to be done with the planting, cultivating and preparing and packaging the seeds. I sell a lot of seeds, and when things are quieter, like now, I give myself a well–earned break to put my feet up and relax by the fire. And I give lectures, horticultural advice. I make a solid living from my work, as do most folk who live in the cottages around here. The Internet allows us to sell the things we make to customers worldwide. Our wee post office is kept busy.'

'It's down by the shops at the harbour, isn't it?'

'Yes. You'll soon get to know everyone. Which reminds me. Ethel has invited you to her cottage for tea. She says to tell you to pop in any time.'

'Ethel?'

'She spins and dyes her own yarn for knitting. I'm not a knitter, but even I can appreciate how beautiful her yarn is. She teaches her skills at the cottage too, and her granddaughter, Glen, is supposed to be coming to stay with her when she's finished her textile course at university.'

'It's very kind of Ethel to invite me. I'll definitely pop in. What cottage belongs to her?'

'The blue one. It's the only cottage with pale blue walls. You can't miss it. She's your nearest neighbour to the north. I'm your second nearest to the south. Others that are close by include the beemaster's cottage and the chocolatier's cottage.'

'A beemaster and a chocolatier?'

'It's a diverse community. A handful of those living here work elsewhere, but most of us don't commute to the big towns or cities. We tend to work from home, to make our living from the things we create, and that's why there's such diversity. Not many of us have the same talents, though the chocolatier is an outsider who moved here to get away from the hustle and bustle of the city. He's still got a shop in the city, but he makes all his new recipes in his cottage.'

He continued to tell me about all the cottage owners. I began to realise I hadn't given enough thought to what my neighbours did for a living. I supposed they worked mainly in farming or fishing. Some did, but there were also very interesting occupants in a few of the cottages.

'Then there's the dressmaker's cottage.'

'Dressmaking? Does she sell fabric? I brought my stash with me to sew quilts but...' I stopped. He was shaking his head.

'The dressmaker keeps herself to herself. She lives alone with her cat, Thimble. Her cottage is difficult to find. It's further inland, in the forest. Quite a trek. That's if you can find it. They say that only those who are invited are welcome.' He shrugged aside the mysterious element. 'But you'll meet everyone else around here that's for sure.'

The storm raged outside. He stood up. 'I'd better get going before I get snowed in and put you in a compromising position by having to stay overnight.'

My heart jolted anxiously at the thought of it.

He put his hood up and headed through to the kitchen. The lights in the cottage flickered for a moment and then returned to normal power.

'A brown out,' he said. 'Not to worry. That lamp will last for hours and you've got the fire going to keep you warm. But if you need me, here's my phone number.'

We exchanged numbers.

'Thanks again for the lamps. It was very thoughtful of you.'

He smiled at me and then opened the kitchen door letting in a gust of freezing air and snow.

He hurried off, again picking his way across the garden, sticking to the path. I'd taken photographs of the garden during my October visit, and had studied them, waiting hopefully for the lease to be mine. In a way, I'd learned the layout of the paths without really trying. Yes, he was avoiding trampling on anything precious. A thoughtful man.

I lost sight of him quickly as the snow sweeping past the kitchen window blurred everything.

I picked up the lamp and took it through to the living room. The power hadn't failed, yet, but I wanted the lamp nearby in case it did.

I sat beside the fire and watched the flames flicker. I was here. I'd actually done what I'd set out to do months ago.

Since arriving, I'd met two good looking men, had one of them in for tea, and been invited to go and visit Ethel. Not bad. Not bad at all.

Although I liked my privacy and could understand that the dressmaker liked hers, I didn't mind that everyone knew my business, that I'd arrived at the cottage and was going to paint and sew. It was probably easier to get to know people here than in the city.

I finally got ready for bed. The fire in the bedroom cast warm shadows on the walls and the ceiling. I watched them as I lay snuggled under one of my handmade quilts in the big, comfy bed. The mattress was so full that I had to climb into bed, but it gave me a view out the window. Through the snow I saw the sea, sparkling like liquid tinsel.

I wore the socks I'd knitted and my fleecy pyjamas, but the fire heated the room and I felt toasty tucked up in bed.

Tomorrow I'd write a letter to my gran telling her all about the cottage, the sea and the snow...and Fintry and Tavion. She was hard of hearing these days, and although my granddad was happy to chat on the phone, my gran preferred reading a letter. 'I'll hear your voice in the words you write, Mairead. I love getting handwritten letters. Everything is emails and text messages these days. I miss the postie delivering a letter, so write me when you find time.'

Find time...

I remembered what Tavion had said. I thought about him and watched the shadows of the fire until I fell asleep.

I slept through the storm and woke up to a breathtaking view — everything white with snow, glistening under a blue sky with the sea in the background.

I jumped out of bed, got washed, dressed, downed a cup of tea and toast, grabbed my artist sketch paper and watercolour pencils and ventured outside to draw.

The light and atmosphere was amazing. I took some photographs, but nothing could compare to sketching the true colours of the scenery and feeling the freshness of the snow and the sea.

After drawing several roughs and a couple of detailed sketches, I tucked my artwork into a shoulder bag and walked down the steps to the shore. I'd always loved snowy days, but I'd never seen a sandy shore covered in pure white snow with the pale grey sea drifting along the coast. I stood there and gazed far out to sea, and any thoughts of whether I'd made a mistake by coming to live at the cottage melted away.

I sketched some more and then started to explore the area, walking first along the snow beside the sea and then heading back up the steps to the cottage. That's when I noticed the lovely blue cottage a fair distance away. Smoke billowed from the chimney pot. Ethel was home. I decided to take her up on her invitation to pop in for a visit.

The cottage reminded me of my gran's old–fashioned, house–shaped biscuit tin. Light shone through the leaded windows. Floral curtains were tied back and the windowsills had ornaments on them. The low–hanging roof dripped with snow, and as I knocked on the front door some of it tumbled down on to my woolly hat and the shoulders of my winter jacket. I brushed it away.

A woman with silvery blonde hair pinned up in a bun, and wearing a knitted lilac shawl around her shoulders, opened the front door and smiled at me.

'Mairead?'

I smiled back at her. 'I heard that a cuppa and a chat was on offer.'

She welcomed me in. I slipped my boots off and left them near the door.

'Sit yourself down by the fire. Your cheeks are rosy, but you look frozen. Grab a blanket from the shelf. There are plenty to choose from.'

She wasn't joking. The shelf was stacked with blankets and shawls, all carefully folded. I assumed these were part of her stock. I didn't like to use any of them.

She grabbed one, a lovely knitted blanket. 'Here, put this over your knees. I'll make the tea.'

The softness of the yarn and intricate stitching of the blanket felt wonderful. I sat down on one of the chairs, placed the blanket over my knees and heated my hands at the fire. I'd dressed for the weather, but the brisk air had chilled me, and the warmth of the fire was very welcome.

Ethel's cottage was a yarn lover's dream house. Skeins of hand dyed yarn were draped in colour coordinated splendour on a display rack at one end of the room. The room itself was an extension of the cottage, so different to the flower hunter's cottage. This was a working house, clearly built to accommodate Ethel's knitting. The colours ranged from neutral shades that echoed the landscape to vibrant turquoise, cerise and deep purples.

Beside the fireside table were two spinning wheels with various types of yarn the colour of sweet peas — pink, cream and lilac.

'Did Tavion give you my message?' she called from the kitchen.

'Yes. He told me when he brought a couple of hurricane lamps over last night due to the storm.'

She carried a tray of tea and shortbread through and placed it on the table.

'Thanks for inviting me,' I said.

She poured the tea. 'I would've invited you personally, but Tavion said he was heading over and would tell you. I'm glad you came. It's nice to meet new people, especially as you're going to be living in the flower hunter's cottage for a year. That's quite a task you've taken on, and I hear that you're planning to paint a lot of the flowers for a book you're writing.'

I helped myself to milk and a piece of the home baked shortbread.

'I illustrated a couple of books for a publisher in London, and when one of his main botanical illustrator's moved to Cornwall and couldn't work regularly for him, he offered me the chance to write and paint a book with floral artwork and designs. I'm a quilter too, you see, and Franklin wants me to create designs that quilters can use for blocks and motifs.'

'It sounds like the type of book I'd love to have.'

'I'll send you a copy once it's published, but that won't be for a while. I'll have moved away by then.'

She stirred a spoon of honey into her tea. 'Maybe you'll stay on here.'

'I can't really do that. The flower hunter will be back home.'

Ethel nodded thoughtfully.

'What's he like?'

'The flower hunter?' Her brows puckered. 'I thought you'd met him.'

I shook my head.

'Didn't he give you the keys to the cottage?'

'No, Fintry gave me the keys.'

She looked at me.

'What?' I said.

'Fintry is the flower hunter.'

'I was told the flower hunter's name was Iain.'

'It is. All the men in that family are called Iain — from Fintry's father to his great grandfather. It's a family tradition to carry the name on. They are, or were, all flower hunters too.'

'His name is Iain, not Fintry?'

'Fintry is his middle name. He goes by that to save having the same name as his father.'

My mind drifted to the golden haired man I'd met. 'So he was the flower hunter?' I sounded wistful.

'He's the type of man who makes quite an impression on the ladies. Very handsome, but hasn't settled down. He's in his early thirties now. His father lives in the Azores these days. Apparently the islands there have fantastic flowers that he's studying. Fintry sails his boat across and visits him at least once a year.'

'Fintry sails to the Azores?'

'All the flower hunters sail. Fintry has a yacht that is moored down at the harbour. Of course, sometimes when he goes off on his treks he will fly from the airport like anyone else. But for shorter trips, he usually sails there.'

'He drove down towards the harbour after giving me the keys to the cottage.'

'Did you notice a large white yacht with blue and white sails?'

'Yes, I did.'

'That's Fintry's boat.'

'Why didn't introduce himself properly?'

'Maybe he thought you knew who he was. Didn't you see pictures of him when you accepted the cottage lease?'

'No, only pictures of the cottage and the garden. I should've looked him up online, but I guess I was so excited about securing the lease and getting things ready to move here.' I paused, then asked, 'Why doesn't Fintry hire someone who lives locally to keep an eye on the cottage while he's away? Not that I'm wishing I hadn't got the lease, it's just that...why hire it out to a stranger when there are local people who could look after it?'

'You've sort of answered your own question. It's less personal to have a stranger, a capable one like yourself, living in the house. To let a neighbour live in the cottage...it's too close to home. Everyone knows everyone else's business, as is usual for a small community like ours, but it's another thing to let them stay in your house and tell every detail to everyone. Far better to let an outsider live there, someone who'll move away after the lease is finished. It's somehow more private.'

I could see she had a point, but I still wished he'd told me who he really was.

I ate my shortbread and we started to chat about her yarn.

'Tavion says you spin and dye the yarn yourself and teach your skills to others.'

'I do. It's important that the old methods aren't lost. My granddaughter, Glen, has become quite the expert at dyeing the yarn.'

'Tavion told me she's coming here once she's finished university.'

Ethel gave me a knowing smile. 'He's sweet on her. He's hoping to ask her out when she comes to learn how to spin the yarn.' She gave a little giggle. 'She doesn't know he fancies her, and I don't want to interfere in case I muck up either of their chances of happiness.' She tapped a finger on the side of her nose. 'So don't let slip I told you.'

'Told me what?'

She laughed. 'Do you have anyone special in your life?'

I explained about my ex being part of the reason why I was here.

'Fresh starts are always exciting.'

'I'm really looking forward to living here.' I told her about my grandparents and about my work. We chatted as if we'd known each other for years.

'Tavion also mentioned about there being a dressmaker who lives in a cottage near here. He didn't tell me her name.'

'No one calls her by name. Everyone knows her simply as the dressmaker. There's only one like her around here. I haven't seen her in a long time. We went to school together. She was always a wee bit...fey.'

'Fey? As in...'

Ethel nodded. 'They say she has the gift. I remember when we were girls. Her father was one of the fishermen. She used to warn him when there was a storm coming hours before anyone else had a hint of bad sailing conditions. She senses things I suppose. An intuitive soul.' Ethel's face took on a thoughtful expression. 'They say her dresses are special because she sews magic into them. I don't know about things like that, but she has film stars who buy her dresses and wear them to special events like film premieres.'

'The dresses she makes must be beautiful.'

'She was always an expert at sewing. Learned from her aunt and grandmother. Nimble fingers and lots of patience to get things right. A perfectionist. A bit like myself, but I never had that extra something that she could stitch into a garment.' She shrugged and tugged her shawl around her shoulders. 'Maybe she does sew magic into the dresses after all.'

CHAPTER THREE

Burgundy Threads

We finished our tea and shortbread, and then Ethel showed me her selection of yarns.

'Are you a knitter, Mairead?'

'I'm more into sewing, especially making quilts, though I love these yarns of yours. If anything starts me knitting again, it'll be your yarns.'

'Come round anytime. Bring your sewing. You can stitch your quilts on my sewing machine. I hardly use it these days. The spinning takes up most of my time. There's increased demand for hand dyed and spun yarn so I'm kept busy with that. And students come along now and then to learn these skills.'

'I'll do that, Ethel.'

'Remember, don't tell Tavion I told you about him being sweet on Glen. I don't want any trouble between him and Fintry.' She spoke as if there had already been trouble between the two men.

'What trouble?'

'You've seen Fintry. Tavion is a fine looking man but Fintry is far more handsome. Fintry's the type of man few women could resist. I thought I caught a flicker of admiration in Glen's eyes when she saw him last summer. Fintry didn't even notice her, and Glen is beautiful. She's a very fashionable girl. I think she's too modern for the likes of Fintry.'

'Did Tavion think that Glen fancied Fintry?'

'No, but they both liked a girl when they were teenagers and she chose Tavion over Fintry. That caused quite a bit of a skirmish. And Tavion has always been a wee bitty jealous of Fintry being a flower hunter. It sounds far more adventurous than a flower grower. Again, when they were younger, Tavion tried to get Fintry's father to teach him about flower hunting but he wouldn't do it.'

'Couldn't Tavion do that himself? After all, he's an expert on flowers.'

'There are methods to flower hunting that are passed on from generation to generation. Skills that Tavion couldn't have learned on his own.'

‘Tavion told me he’s happy to be at home and not travelling all over the world.’

‘I believe he is, but there’s this male rivalry at the core of their friendship and I don’t think it’ll ever be resolved.’

‘I won’t mention any of this to Tavion, and I hope things work out for him with Glen.’

‘They’d make a fine couple, but I’ll never interfere in matters of the heart, especially given my past romance with a man I thought would be the love of my life. When I was young, life felt different. I followed my heart and got it broken before I found the man who really was meant for me.’

I encouraged her to tell me about him.

‘I was only nineteen at the time. Fintry’s grandfather was barely twenty, but oh, he was a fine looking man even at that age.’

‘You dated Fintry’s grandfather?’

Ethel nodded. ‘I fell in lust with him the first time I saw him one hot summer’s day. He stood on the bow of his father’s boat and dived into the sea, bare chest, wearing only his trousers. I watched him swim along the shore and then he walked out of the sea, all glistening wet torso, lean and fit.’ She sighed even now at the memory. ‘I’d never felt like that before. He saw me watching him and smiled at me. I couldn’t stop blushing and ran off up to the cottage. I’d moved in with my parents that summer.’

‘I thought you were born and brought up here.’ She seemed to fit in so perfectly.

‘No, I was born in Falkirk. My parents moved here when my father inherited the cottage from his uncle. I was already a young woman, and Fintry’s grandfather was my first love. My mother called it a girlish crush, but I knew it was more than that. The flower hunters are all extremely handsome men and I defy any young lass in my time not to have fallen under his sexy spell.’

‘Did he ask you out on a date?’

‘No, he walked up to the door of my cottage and asked my mother to tell me there was a dance that night down at the harbour and that I should wear a pretty dress and come and dance with him.’

‘He had a cheek.’

‘He did. My mother and I joked about it. I said I had no intention of jumping to his tune, but as the evening wore on and the music wafted up from the harbour we both thought — what harm would it do to go along and enjoy the dancing?'

'And so you went?'

'I did. I wore a dress I'd made and there was no silver in my hair then. The sun had lightened it to a golden blonde that rivalled his blond locks. Everyone said we suited each other, as a couple, and for a wee while things were great. Then he had to sail off with his father, promising he'd write to me, making all sorts of promises that he loved me and we'd have a future together when he returned.' She sighed again, this time with sadness. 'He was away for nearly two years. I waited. There wasn't a man to match him, not round here, except for a boy who was the complete opposite of him — dark haired and strong and sturdy. He worked as a joiner. The dependable sort and he kept asking me out.'

'Did you go out with him?'

'No, I waited on a flower hunter who came home with a young woman he'd met when they'd been living in London. Apparently, the flowers they found had to be authenticated and officially logged, and he'd met her and fell in love with her. When he sailed back I went down to the harbour to see him and there he was with her. He shrugged his shoulders at me, smiled and then walked right past me holding her hand. And that was that.'

'That's horrible.'

'I was upset, and it was my parents who encouraged me to go to a birthday party near here. The joiner was there and...I realised that the man who was meant for me was the one who was there all along. We got married the following year and were married for a long time before he passed away.'

I felt quite teary hearing her story.

'Don't upset yourself, Mairead. We were happy. And the flower hunter never married that girl. He was a brilliant hunter, but unreliable when it came to love and responsibility. I was lucky.'

'Do you think all the men in that family are unreliable in love?'

'Fintry doesn't seem to date many girls. He's always working, focusing on his career, so I don't know. What I do know is that Tavion wants to settle down with Glen and he's picked the wrong woman.'

'She's not attracted to him?'

Ethel pulled her shawl around her. 'It's not so much that as...Glen is ambitious. She wants to have a career in the fashion world, as a designer, and she has the talent for it. She wants to travel to New York and Paris. Tavion wants a wife who'll be happy to live here.'

'Doesn't he understand that Glen wants more than to live with him at his cottage?'

'I've tried to tell him, without interfering or ruining things for him. He comes by to help out. He's a thoughtful man, but I know he also wants to hear any news I have about Glen. How's she getting on? When is she coming back? And I tell him — Glen is off to see the fashions in London and she's hoping one day to work in New York.'

'You'd think he'd take the hint.'

'Tavion needs to look for someone else, someone attainable. Glen's not the one for him. I don't think so anyway. I could be wrong, but he'd never be happy trailing after her around the world to fashion shows. She's coming to learn how to spin the yarn so she understands all aspects of the textile trade and plans to have her own brand of fabrics and yarns.'

'That is ambitious. Good luck to her.'

'She'll need it because it's a fine career she's aiming for but a harsh life too.' Ethel gave me a resigned smile. 'Glen has to do what's right for her. The last thing I want to do is influence her. I've already taught her everything I know about dyeing the yarn. I'll teach her how to spin it. Then Glen has to decide what she wants to do with that knowledge, but at least it'll be another person who can carry on the skills. The skills won't be lost and that's important.'

I wandered over to where a selection of yarn was draped. 'I love the colours you've used. They're really beautiful.'

'Thank you. I try to divide the spectrum into all the neutral tones. Some of the yarn is completely its natural colour.' She held up a skein of oatmeal coloured yarn. 'Others have a mixture of dyes I've developed over the years.'

I ran my fingers down the length of a deep blue yarn. 'I love this blue.'

'The artist in you will appreciate how the values and tones complement the range of yarns.'

I nodded, and admired the skeins of burgundy yarn. The colour was intense.

'I based those tones on one of the plants in my garden — burgundy threads.'

'I know that flower,' I told her, continuing to look around.

'I have a website,' she announced. 'I never thought I'd take to techie computer stuff, but you have to go with the flow of the world. I'm a silver surfer.'

I laughed. 'I bet your yarn is popular.' I couldn't imagine it wouldn't be. It was so lovely.

'I sell to customers all over the country these days. It's so handy that I can do it all from this wee cottage.'

I wondered about her daughter.

'She moved away years ago. Married a businessman from Devon. We keep in touch by phone. She rarely comes up to visit me so I'm always happy when Glen comes to stay. I enjoy the company. Another cup of tea before you go?' she offered.

I ended up staying for lunch — a bowl of potato soup sprinkled with chives and another piece of Ethel's shortbread — and having a go at spinning the yarn. It was tricky at first then I started to get the feel for it.

'Did you ever think when you moved to the cottage you'd end up staying here all these years?' I asked her while I untangled some of the fibres.

'No. I thought I'd end up living in one of the bigger towns near here, or the city, and visit my parents at the cottage.' She glanced out the window at the view. Flakes of snow fell lightly in the breeze. 'But there's something about living here that's so perfect. The seasons are defined. The people are genuine, even the grouchy ones. I like the sense of community, and I loved working with my mother, working with the yarns, knitting and all the crafting life that went with it. I realised I didn't want to leave. I had everything I needed and loved.' She smiled and recalled an anecdote. 'A few months after we arrived, my mother decided to paint the cottage pale blue to make it different from the other cottages. It was originally whitewashed. Most of them are white or have unpainted stonework. Anyway, what an uproar that caused. There were pursed lips and disapproval all round.'

'Why?'

'People don't like change. They like things to look the same way. They didn't approve of our cottage being blue, even if it was the palest blue that matched the sea on a summery day.'

'Did you have to change it?'

'No, my mother was always of the mind that she would do what she wanted, what we liked as a family. Eventually, when people got to know us, they stopped screwing their noses up at the paintwork and it was all forgotten. Years later, I had a notion to try and make things right, and I had the cottage painted white again. Well, that caused a furore all over again.'

'Why would they object to you painting it white to match the other cottages?'

'It had been blue for decades and everyone was so used to it they didn't want it any other colour. People get set in their ways. Despite all the modernisation and stuff that goes on around us, people like to feel comfortable with what's familiar. It feels safer. So I had it painted blue again and it's been that colour ever since.'

A wave of emotion went through me. 'It's not easy to let go of what's familiar.'

She knew what I meant. 'Will that ex boyfriend of yours come looking for you here?'

'No, it's over.'

She nodded thoughtfully. 'You came to the right place to mend a broken heart. Maybe you'll find a man locally who is better suited to you.'

'I'm not looking for romance. I'm not looking for anyone.'

'That's often when you find them, or they find you.'

I thanked Ethel again for inviting me, for lunch and for showing me how to spin the yarn — and for making me feel less alone in the world when I was far from home.

I headed back to the cottage and wrote a letter to my gran. I took it down to the post office. The afternoon light cast a shimmer across the sea. The snow still covered the shore, but I imagined how it must've looked that summer's day when Ethel saw Fintry's grandfather dive into the water. The flower hunters sounded like an adventurous family of men. I wondered where Fintry was sailing to on his yacht. The Azores to visit his father? Far across the sea to where a new species of plant had been seen? I'd assumed he lived locally and I'd see him around the area, but now I knew he was the flower hunter, there seemed little chance of that.

I posted my letter, met the postmaster who told me my letter would arrive within two days, and then wandered down to the harbour's edge to gaze out at the sea. I hoped my time living here would be happy. I closed my eyes for a moment and wished that things would work out well.

When I opened them I saw a black cat sitting on the harbour wall. It wore a collar with a little silver thimble hanging from it. I swear its curious green eyes looked at me, and then it jumped down on to the shore.

I hurried to see where it went, but all I could see were a few tiny paw prints in the snow. No sign of the cat. No sign at all.

CHAPTER FOUR

Candytuft Needlepoint

I set up my artwork on a table at the front window of the living room. Light shone in from the sea as I painted some of the drawings I'd sketched. I painted in watercolours, working with a palette of blues and neutral shades.

When the natural light coming in the window faded I flicked on my daylight bulb lamp, adjusting it so it showed the true colours of my paints on the watercolour paper.

I'd lit the fire, and the room felt cosy to work in. The table was quite long and I planned to keep it set up for my artwork at this end of the living room, along with my laptop, while my sewing machine was at the opposite end with a view of the back garden. Behind me, the fire glowed in the hearth and there were comfy chairs and a sofa to relax on while unwinding after a busy day.

I would've kept on painting if it hadn't been for the constant rumblings of my stomach protesting that I hadn't made dinner or eaten anything since lunch with Ethel. I went through to the kitchen to cook the potatoes and turnip I'd bought at the post office. Yes, although there was a little grocery shop at the harbour, the post office had a supply of food items, including tatties and neeps. The postmaster had told me they were fresh in that day, suggested I boil them up and mash them to make 'thump' and serve with gravy. Sold. I bought them along with a tin of cocoa and a packet of biscuits I hadn't eaten in years. Maybe it was the effect of being on my own, let loose to munch whatever I wanted. It had to be a good sign that buying cocoa, something I hadn't had in ages, filled me with glee. Simple pleasures were always the most satisfying.

While the vegetables boiled I stoked the fire and had a look at my artwork. Then I remembered about the folders filled with the flower hunting sketches. I flicked through them and selected several to paint later on after dinner. I didn't plan to use the actual drawings, just to see the construction of each flower — the real shape and size of the petals along with its floral data. It was fascinating to read their history, where they'd come from originally, often decades ago from the other side of the world, and how they'd adapted to thrive in their new home. And of course to learn about the flower hunters who'd ventured to find them. Men like the ones who'd lived in the cottage. Men like Fintry. It was quite a thought to somehow be a small part of that history, to contribute some of my floral artwork.

The bubbling of the pot on the stove reminded me of dinner. I ran through, drained the water off, mashed the potatoes and turnip together and served it up with lashings of gravy. Yummy.

After clearing everything away, I sat back down and continued to paint by the glow of my lamp. Candytuft 'needlepoint' flowers were painted in pink and purple watercolours. I also designed a motif for my book that needlepoint embroiderers could use for sewing.

A note had been added by Fintry stating the candytuft featured had come from the beemaster's cottage garden and the flowers were a favourite with his bees. These little snippets of information held my interest. I wondered if I should tell Franklin about the existence of these folders of work. He would perhaps be interested in publishing them. They were so different to my book which was geared more for the quilter, the crafter and those who loved embroidery. The flower hunter folders included layers of history right up to the present day. The sketches reminded me of those fairytale books, faded in parts, splashes of ink gone astray. The real flower photographs were featured in seasons from the first snowdrops to sunflowers and Christmas roses. They had everything. So beautiful. Yes, I'd definitely mention this to Franklin when I spoke to him. I'd promised to call him with an update on the book's progress. I didn't mind. Franklin was such a gentleman, a fatherly type, with a sharp mind for the publishing business and a kind heart for his authors and illustrators.

Throughout the folders there was very little mention of the women in the flower hunters' lives. According to Ethel, Fintry's mother split up with his father when he was just a boy. When asked to choose between living in Dundee with his mother or staying with his father, Fintry chose the latter, later regretting that his mother had become estranged from the family.

I flicked to the back of a folder. A scattering of postcards, faded with age, many dating back to Fintry's grandfather's era, were all that existed of notes home to the wives who were waiting for their adventurous men.

After painting the candytuft I attempted to capture the delicacy of the snowdrops. I used white gouache along with the watercolours.

I don't know where the time went, but suddenly it felt really late. There wasn't a clock in the cottage. Not one. Another reminder that clock watching wasn't part of the lifestyle here. Ethel had summed it up earlier when the subject cropped up.

'What time were you up this morning?' she'd asked me.

'Early. Around seven.' I'd probably sounded rather proud of myself. Up at the crack of dawn after several sleepless nights in the city, anxious about my decision to live in the cottage and then driving for hours through the snow to get there.

Ethel pressed her lips together firmly and said, 'Ask me what time I got up.'

'Okay. What time did you get up, Ethel?'

She shrugged casually. 'I've no idea. Early I suppose. The morning was still dark when I made my porridge. But that's the thing, Mairead. I'm not saying you can't watch the time when you need to for appointments and normal things, however, if you really want to feel better and make the most of living here, let yourself unwind. Sleep when you're tired. Don't force yourself to stay up late. Go to bed. Get a cosy night's sleep. Wake when you wake, not when an alarm tells you to. Don't jangle your nerves with stuff like that. Gradually, your body will adjust to the way of things naturally. Maybe you're an early riser and you don't know it. Perhaps you're the type who thrives staying up late and watching the stars in the night sky. And maybe, just maybe, you're like most of us around here. We wake quite early, get on with our day, and go to bed at a decent hour. When you enjoy that balance, time slows down and you won't need to watch the clock. Time will stretch out and an afternoon will feel like an afternoon should. Relaxing after lunch and with lots of time to do various things before dinner. Your world will become settled and there will be more time for everything.'

I washed my paint brushes and tidied my artwork table ready for work the following day. I was tempted to check the time on my phone but decided not to. It was late, bedtime. I put my phone away.

The fire still flickered in the hearth, more embers than flames. I intended getting ready for bed and didn't want to waste any more fuel on it, so I left it to glow and boiled the kettle to make a mug of cocoa. It was so long since I'd made it I had to check the tin for instructions. That's when I saw lights outside in the darkness. Several people were carrying lamps like the lamps Tavion had given me. In fact...there he was. It looked like they were out searching for someone.

I put on my boots, woolly hat and jacket, lit one of the lamps I'd stored in the kitchen, and ventured outside to see what was going on.

Tavion trudged across the snow towards me. 'Thimble's gone missing. We're out looking for him.'

'Can I help?' I offered.

'No, it's fine. We've searched everywhere.' He gazed up at the threatening dark sky. 'More snow is heading this way. We'll have to give up soon, but thanks.'

'You can't give up. I saw him earlier, down by the harbour.'

Tavion shook his head. 'It couldn't have been the dressmaker's cat. He never goes near the sea. Doesn't like water. It must've been another cat.'

'No, it was him. He had a collar with a little silver thimble on it.'

A couple of people stopped on hearing this. My voice carried in the cold night air.

'Are you sure?' the postmaster shouted over to me. 'I've never seen him near the harbour.'

'His fur was black, a black cat, and he had huge green eyes.'

Tavion turned and nodded to them. 'I'll go down and have a look. You head home before the snow gets heavier.'

The postmaster and one of the other men offered to join him, but Tavion insisted they get back safely to their houses.

'I'll go with you,' I said to Tavion.

He could tell from my expression I was determined to help.

'Okay. This shouldn't take long.'

We walked together through the snow, past my cottage and down to the harbour.

'Where did you see him?'

I pointed. 'Over there on the wall. He jumped down on to the shore and then...'

'What?'

I felt he might think me odd as I said, 'He disappeared. There were paw prints in the snow but no sign of the cat. I thought it was very...unusual.'

'He's the dressmaker's cat,' he said, as if this explained everything.

Waves hit off the shore and for the first time I sensed a dangerous vibe in the air.

Tavion looked up at the sky again and referred to the approaching snow storm. 'It's going to be a fierce one. We need to be quick. You search that way. I'll check the anchoring bay.'

We split up, like we'd done this a hundred times, both knowing what the other meant and heading back to where we began at the same time. In sync.

The muscles in Tavion's face were tight with concern and from the cold wind blasting in from the sea. 'There's no sign of him.'

I glanced back and forth. He had to be hiding somewhere. Sheltering. In desperation I called out, 'Thimble.' My voice was blown away in the wind. Had the cat even heard me when I could barely hear myself?

'He doesn't answer to his name,' said Tavion.

I looked up at him, eyes blinking against the blustering wind. 'He doesn't come down to the harbour either, does he?' I held on to my woolly hat, almost losing it in one of the sweeping gusts.

Tavion nodded at my counter argument and then shouted with manly power against the storm. His voice carried across the harbour wall. 'Thimble. THIMBLE.'

Nothing.

We started to walk away as if our boots were weighted with lead. We'd tried. We'd really tried.

'Meow.'

'Did you hear that?' I said to Tavion, stopping suddenly to listen. The sound was so faint I wondered if it was my imagination.

'I didn't hear anything.' Tavion put an arm around my shoulder, encouraging me to walk on.

'Meow.'

This time it was louder and we both turned around at the sound to see the cat sitting on the harbour wall.

Tavion handed me his lamp and hurried over. I expected the cat to run away, but no, it waited to be lifted, tucked into his jacket and carried safely. Its face peered out at me, eyes again filled with curiosity. What was it thinking?

Tavion walked me back to my cottage and then continued on, carrying his lamp and the cat, towards the forest.

I wanted to shout to him, 'Will you be okay?' Somehow I knew he would. Tavion and the cat.

I'd no idea what time it was. Later than late. Well past bedtime. After lighting the fire in the bedroom, I made a mug of cocoa and climbed into bed without spilling it.

Propped up on two fluffy pillows, and wearing ridiculous fleecy jim–jams, I sipped my cocoa and watched the fire flicker. I would miss this when I had to leave and go back to the city, which was a silly thought because I'd only just arrived and had an entire year at the cottage. But still...nights like this would last forever in my memory.

I'd just finished drinking my cocoa when I heard someone knock on the back door.

'Mairead. It's me,' Tavion shouted.

I jumped out of bed and ran through to the kitchen, unbolted the door and let him in. He carried a brown paper parcel. He shook the snow off it and handed it to me. 'Sorry to come round so late. I saw your lights were still on and thought I'd hand this in. The dressmaker asked me to give it to you by way of thanks for helping to find Thimble.'

I accepted the parcel which was tied with string. It felt reasonably heavy and yet quite soft. I'd no idea what it was. 'She didn't need to give me a present.'

He gave me a knowing look. 'She had it already wrapped for you.'

'How could she...? I mean, how would she have known?'

Tavion shrugged. 'Some things don't have an explanation.'

I gazed for a moment at the parcel. 'Should I open it now?'

'Yes. She asked me to wait while you opened it.'

'Why? Not that I mind.'

He motioned towards the parcel. 'Open it.'

I put it on the kitchen table, untied the string and started to unwrap whatever was inside.

'It's fabric,' I squealed with delight. 'A bundle of beautiful fabric.'

Tavion smiled at me and watched as I held up the various fabrics, like sample pieces, of gorgeous cottons and silks. Each piece was a fat quarter, about the size of a pillow case. A few were longer and not quite so wide, and as I laid them on the table I realised the longer strips fitted together to form what looked like the makings of a landscape art quilt, something I'd always wanted to attempt but never had.

'The dressmaker must've heard that I'm a quilter. These are perfect for quilting. So, so beautiful...' My words trailed off as I saw the folded piece of fabric underneath them all. Oyster silk glistened with metallic thread and beads. There had to be at least two metres of it. 'Wow, this is gorgeous.' I unfolded it carefully, realising there was a lot more to it than two metres, several perhaps. The silk was so fine that even encrusted with embellishments it folded easily into a small bundle.

Tavion watched me carefully, as if waiting for something. My reaction? Well, he could see I was delighted with the fabric. I held up the oyster silk, admiring it glitter under the kitchen light. 'This looks magical.' Then I realised. 'In fact, it looks like vintage fabric. Yes, it's vintage, isn't it?' I asked, surmising he knew about it.

'It is.'

I studied it. 'This has already been sewn and worn as a garment. What was it? A dress?'

Tavion knew, waiting on me saying the words. 'The dressmaker asked me not to prompt you. She wanted to know if you understood.'

And suddenly I did. 'This was once a wedding dress, wasn't it?'

He nodded. 'She'll be pleased you like it. I know as much about fabric and sewing as I do about knitting, but that looks beautiful to me.'

I felt the richness of the silk as I folded it carefully. 'I'd like to thank her.'

'She doesn't have visitors.'

'She spoke to you.'

'At the doorstep of her cottage when I gave her Thimble. It was an exchange. I handed her the cat and she gave me the parcel.'

'If she wanted you to gauge my reaction, how will she ever know?'

'There's a woman who lives locally who helps tend to the cottage, does her shopping, that sort of thing. The dressmaker asked me to pass a message to her.'

'Fair enough. Tell her...tell her I love all the fabric. I'll make quilts with it and keep the glittery silk for something special.'

'She said you'd know what to do with it when the time came.'

'Well, thanks for bringing it.'

We gazed at each other for a moment.

'I'd better be going. There's not much left of this night and we both need some sleep.' He opened the kitchen door. 'Goodnight, Mairead.'

'Goodnight. Thanks again.'

I closed the door and went back to bed, grateful for the warmth of the fire. The room was toasty and welcoming. I fell asleep within minutes despite having a hundred thoughts running through my mind.

In the middle of the night a loud knock woke me up. I looked out the bedroom window. Perhaps it was the storm hitting off the cottage? It was snowing, and the strong wind had created drifts across the landscape like frozen waves from the sea.

There it was again. Loud and insistent.

Wearing my pyjamas and knitted socks I padded through to the lounge and peered out the window to see who it was.

What was he doing here? Was something wrong?

I hurried through and opened the front door. Snow blew around him and fluttered inside the hallway.

I looked at him standing there — winter coat, boots, gloves, dressed for the weather, but no sensible man would be chapping on my door in the middle of a stormy night. Would they?

'Can I come in, Mairead?'

I stepped aside, holding the door open for him. 'It's your cottage.'

CHAPTER FIVE

Tea Roses

'I apologise for not introducing myself properly when we met,' he said, taking off his long, dark, weather–beaten coat and hanging it up on a peg in the hallway. He wore black trousers with lots of zip pockets, a black jumper and boots that matched his coat. He brought the scent of snow and fresh air in with him as he followed me into the living room.

The fire had lost all its heat, but seeing this handsome man standing there sent a surge of warmth through my whole body. It was unexpected and unwelcome, especially when I turned to face him, to challenge him for keeping his identity a secret when it seemed to be totally unnecessary.

The air sizzled between us. He knew a confrontation was due, not only for being sneaky, but for now turning up when he was supposed to be away on his travels abroad. And there was the horrible thought I'd be turfed out now he was back. I would argue that the lease was signed and we'd made an agreement.

'I need to ask you a favour,' he began. 'I need you to promise not to tell anyone I'm here. Everyone thinks I've sailed to the Azores and then on to other parts of Europe.'

'You want me to lie? I don't even know you. And what am I supposed to do now? Just pack my bags and go back to the city and keep my mouth shut?'

He eyed my pyjamas. Hardly the outfit to wear to be taken seriously. Was there a hint of admiration in those stunning green eyes of his that I was prepared to challenge him? Or was it simply the effort to suppress a smirk?

'Say it,' I told him.

'Say what?'

I glared at him. He knew fine what I meant.

'Your eh...nightwear is very practical. Surprising for a city girl. Usually they never dress for the weather or the terrain.'

'Really? I suppose from your extensive knowledge you're used to city girls frequenting your cottage in their nightwear.'

'No. You're the first.' He sighed and ran a hand through his already ruffled blond hair. 'It's just that sometimes we have holidaymakers in the area, young women, fashionable sorts like yourself, who wear tottering heeled shoes and fancy boots to navigate the terrain. And in the colder months they're always frozen. Fashionable but frozen.'

I wondered if by chance he was including Glen in his sweeping statement.

'Thankfully, I had the common sense to pop into a mountaineering shop in Edinburgh on my way here. The owner, Matt, kitted me out with sturdy boots, jacket, thermals, everything I needed apart from these pyjamas which were something I'd bought last winter. Even in the city the nights are cold.' I took a deep breath and then added, 'What did you expect I'd be wearing in bed? Jeans and a nice jumper? These are pyjamas. They're supposed to be silly, frivolous and cosy.'

'You're angry with me, aren't you?'

'Angry? Why would I be angry? You don't tell me you're the flower hunter, that you own the cottage as you hand the keys to me, then you turn up in the middle of the night asking me to lie for you — and I suppose, renege on the lease.'

He shook his head adamantly. 'No, that's not why I'm here. The lease agreement stands as promised.'

My eyes widened. 'You don't expect me to share the cottage with you? Hide you under the bed and squirrel food in for you.'

He laughed. 'You really are angry with me.'

'And that amuses you?' I was tired. Very tired, and out of sorts for various reasons, from disappearing cats, mysterious dressmakers, no peace since I'd arrived in the cottage and unwanted feelings for a man I was angry with. Damn him for being so bloomin' handsome — and sexy. Sexy as hell actually. Damn him again.

'You're cursing me under your breath, aren't you?'

'Don't tell me you've got the gift as well.'

'Ah, you've met the dressmaker.'

'No, but I helped find her cat tonight. Tavion and the others were out looking for him.'

'You have been busy.'

'Maybe I should go back to the city where it's quieter.'

He sat down on the sofa, and even sitting there he seemed tall. 'Don't be mad at me, Mairead. I have my reasons for doing things.'

I stood my ground, waiting to hear these reasons. 'Well, what are they?'

'Could we discuss it over a cup of tea?'

I nodded, went through to the kitchen and clicked the kettle on. Fintry followed me. I started to set two cups up when I realised he was staring at the fabric bundle I'd left lying on the table. The sparkling fabric was on the top.

Fintry glared at it and then at me. 'Where did you get this?'

'The dressmaker sent it to me for helping find Thimble. She gave it to Tavion to give to me.'

The mention of Tavion seemed to add fuel to his simmering anger.

I grabbed the fabric and went to fold the whole bundle away in the brown paper, but he put his hand on mine to stop me.

I gazed up at him. 'What's wrong with the fabric? Do you recognise it?'

A sadness filled his eyes. 'Yes, that was once my mother's wedding dress. The fabric was specially woven for her locally.'

I could see this distressed him. I pulled my hand away slowly and wrapped the fabric up in the paper. 'I'll put this out of the way for now, then I'll make the tea and you can tell me what you're up to.'

I put the fabric in the wardrobe and came back through to the kitchen. Fintry had started to make our tea so I let him. We took it through to the living room and sat down opposite each other.

'As I said,' he began, 'I have my reasons for wanting to keep things quiet. There have been hints of a new species of flower and various flower hunters are after it. But it's not abroad. It's here in Scotland.'

'Here?'

He nodded. 'Near a hidden valley. I'm hoping to spend the next few weeks searching for it, but if anyone around here knew about this, it would soon be picked up by the media. The newspapers would pester us. We've had the media causing chaos here a few times over the years. It upsets a lot of the people who live locally. I need to keep this quiet until I find the flower.'

'Won't the press come here then anyway?'

'No, once the story breaks and a press release is sent out with all the information and photographs they need, they'll publish the news and then not bother with us. That's how it usually works. I'm simply trying to avoid our quiet community being in the spotlight of the media. I let people think I was sailing abroad. I would've already been gone, but the lease manager genuinely couldn't get here so I had to give you the keys.'

'Where is your boat? How did you get here tonight? Won't people see it anchored at the harbour?'

'I left the boat in a harbour further up the coast. I'm staying in a farmhouse that belongs to trusted friends while they're on holiday. My plans are to use that as a base and head back and forth, searching for the new species. I obviously won't find anything because of all this snow, so while I'm at the farmhouse, I thought I'd get on with some of my writing and research. I left my files here. With all the fuss of the lease manager I forgot to take them with me.'

'So you're back for your paperwork and stuff and then going to live in the farmhouse?'

'Yes. All I need you to do is not tell anyone about this.'

'Okay.'

'You'll keep this quiet? You won't even tell Ethel?'

'How did you know I'd met Ethel?'

'When she heard I'd leased the cottage out to a woman who loved to paint and sew she was delighted. She said she was looking forward to meeting you.'

'She invited me over for tea. I like Ethel.'

'Me too, but she's an awful gossip. Kind but...well...she'd tell everyone what I was up to.'

'I won't say a thing.'

'Thank you.'

He downed the rest of his tea. 'Here's my phone number in case you need to contact me.'

I gave him my number and my email.

He put his coat on, gathered the paperwork he'd forgotten which was in the smaller bedroom drawers that I hadn't even looked in, and got ready to leave.

'I got your note, on the folder,' I said. 'I'd be happy to contribute some floral artwork.'

'That would be great. We'll settle the finances when the lease is up.'

I nodded and then said, 'Have you ever thought of publishing the information that's in the folders. It makes for fascinating reading and there's a sort of vintage quality to them that's very appealing.'

'No, I've never considered it.'

'You should. I could mention it to my publisher. He's very open to new ideas.'

Fintry looked at me. 'Yes, do that. Perhaps we can come to some sort of arrangement.'

I smiled at him. From being angry with him, attracted to him and then considering getting him a publishing deal, my emotions were all over the place.

He smiled back at me, opened the door and stepped out into the cold night. Before walking away he leaned down and kissed me, briefly, softly, but I felt the heat rush through me. From his expression, he sensed it too.

'Thank you again, Mairead.' And then he hurried off.

If he'd wanted to leave a lasting impression, he'd certainly done that. I closed the door and leaned against it. Wow. Just wow.

I was prepared to feel bleary eyed at breakfast, but instead I felt quite perky — and hungry. All the fresh sea air had given me a healthy appetite. It was the sea air I told myself as I cooked two slices of French toast, and not the effects from last night with Fintry. One kiss didn't mean anything. Nothing. He was grateful. It was just a kiss.

Trying not to think about kissing Fintry, I finished breakfast and then started work, painting tea roses. I transferred detailed drawings I'd finished months ago on to watercolour paper. My portfolio was filled with sketches, ready for painting. I'd been drawing since the previous year, especially during the summer, gathering all the flowers I needed for my book. The actual paintings, either in watercolours, oils, pastels or acrylics were the things I had to work on while I was here at the cottage. The content of my book had been agreed with Franklin, depicting the seasons, vintage flowers, heritage plants, basically a beautifully illustrated book of floral artwork and snippets of information about the flowers. Design motifs and templates for quilting and embroidery were to be included in the book.

I gazed out at the snow covering the garden. I loved the snow and yet I was eager to see what the garden looked like in spring and summer. The lists of flowers in Fintry's folders included many that I'd drawn — delphiniums, fuchsia, cosmos, heliotrope, snapdragons, peonies, hydrangeas and pansies.

The great thing about the wintry weather was that it gave me a chance to forge ahead with the artwork. By the time the snow faded and spring emerged, I'd be well ahead with my deadline. This would let me concentrate on looking after the garden.

When I finished painting the tea roses I had the notion to paint the cottage in one of the pictures. I ran outside and snapped several photographs of the cottage in the snow, from various angles, some with the sea, others showing the trees in the garden, their branches pared to the bone and iced white with frost and snow.

I ran back inside, kicked my boots off, put my knitted slipper socks on, and viewed the photos on my laptop. They were stunning. If I could capture even half of their beauty in my artwork I would be delighted.

I stopped for lunch, just a bowl of tomato soup and bread, which I ate in the kitchen. If I'd thought to buy flour at the post office, I'd have baked some scones, something I could rustle up in jig time.

Then I heard the ping of an email on my laptop in the living room. I checked the name of the sender — Fintry. I read the message.

When I was making the tea last night, I couldn't help noticing that you had very little food in the kitchen, so look out for a delivery around lunchtime today. They deliver my groceries regularly. I'd cancelled them because I was letting out the cottage, but I've told them to continue with the deliveries as normal. They're on me. Hope this helps in some way to make up for you being angry with me. They'll give you a list of their grocery items so that you can make your own selection for the next delivery.

The peep of a horn made me look up from the laptop. A large van parked outside. The driver jumped out, opened the van doors, and started to carry bags of shopping to the front door.

'Would you like me to carry them through to the kitchen?' he said.

'Eh, yes, thank you.'

He seemed to know his way around the cottage better than I did and even put the frozen food in bulk in the freezer.

Oh yes, I could get used to this type of living.

'Fintry off on his travels abroad again?' the man said.

'He is. I'm leasing the cottage while he's away.'

'I got an email from him telling me to continue with the deliveries. Here's a list of what goods I offer. You can order through the website if you're online.'

'That would be handy.'

He went back and forth bringing in all the bags. 'Okay, that's everything. See you next time, Mairead.'

And off he went. He'd even delivered fuel for the fire which was kept outside near the garden shed.

I smiled to myself. Within fifteen minutes the bare cupboards had been filled. I peered inside the store cupboard and there was a bag of flour, baking power, bicarbonate of soda and dried fruit. I could bake scones. And there were jars of strawberry and bramble jam. Oh, I was definitely baking scones.

The oven soon heated up the kitchen and the aroma of home baking wafted through the cottage.

I looked to see what else Fintry had ordered. Fresh vegetables, fruit, garlic, lemon juice, ginger, tomato sauce, mayonnaise, olive oil, sea salt, black pepper, stock cubes, mustard, lentils, oats, pasta, tinned goods, custard, sugar, milk, butter, eggs, cheese, whipped cream and dark chocolate. This man knew how to shop. If he'd included fish fingers and chips in the freezer I'd let his regular order stand. I peeked inside. Yes, he'd bought those along with chicken, mince, frozen veg and frozen raspberries. Pavlova here I come.

When the scones were ready I sat at my art table enjoying a freshly baked scone, still warm from the oven, smothered in whipped cream and strawberry jam. Mmmm, scrumptious. Fintry was a bad influence on me. All this delicious food, stolen kisses and asking me to lie for him. I never thought that life at the cottage would be quite so...enticing.

I replied to his email.

The groceries arrived. Thanks. The cupboards are no longer bare, and I'm now munching a freshly baked scone and thinking about having fish fingers and chips for dinner when I should be working. You are a bad influence on me.

In more ways than one, but I didn't mention that.

An email pinged back. *Glad you're not going hungry. Enjoy your scone. Sorry to be a bad influence. I could say the same about you. I'm ordering groceries and emailing you when I should be halfway up a mountainside.*

I smiled to myself and then got on with my painting, determined to finish the watercolour delphiniums in gorgeous shades of blue before the natural light faded.

In the late afternoon an email arrived from Franklin in London asking how I was getting on at the cottage.

I replied telling him the artwork was ahead of schedule due to being holed up in the cottage and that I'd definitely meet the deadline. I also mentioned about the flower hunter folders as a proposed book and attached a couple of sample pages to let him see the style of it. His publishing company specialised in non–fiction, highly illustrated books, particularly those with a botanical theme.

Franklin emailed within the hour. *I'm interested in the flower hunter material. I've shown the sample pages to marketing and discussed this with one of my editors. I like the idea and want to take things further. It seems more like an editorial job than anything else, and deciding what to leave in and what to take out. But I like the feel of it, the sense of history and generations of flower hunters in Fintry's family. Without wishing to jeopardise your time working on your own book, scan what's in the folders and email it to me. I'll take it from there. Usual fee. Well done, Mairead. Speak soon.*

I felt so excited and immediately began scanning in the pages, just as I did with my own artwork, and emailed Fintry before pressing the send button. Fintry confirmed I should send it, though I doubted he understood the book publishing process and that he was on the brink of getting a deal.

I pressed send.

Then I made a tasty dinner, popping a tray of chips and fish fingers in the oven while I sorted bread and condiments to go with it. Sweet red pepper chutney? Yes, Fintry could do my shopping anytime.

Afterwards, I fell asleep on the sofa listening to the crackling fire and sounds of the snow storm swirling around the little cottage while I was safe and snug inside.

CHAPTER SIX

Old–Fashioned Four O'Clocks

I painted old–fashioned four o'clock flowers at around nine in the evening after waking up feeling more content than I had in months. I had a list of flowers that needed to be painted, and rather than skip from one to the other, I planned to work my way through the list for each chapter of my book. With the tea roses and delphiniums finished earlier, the little trumpet–shaped four o'clocks were next.

My colour palate had sunshine yellows, magenta, orange and white and I even painted the striped variety. I'd drawn these during the summer. They grew in my grandparents garden and were evening bloomers that smelled of sweet lemons. I painted a couple of extra four o'clocks on a small piece of watercolour paper and when it was dry I put it in an envelope to send to my gran with my next letter.

The flower illustrations were reasonably small. Each one fitted on to an A4 sheet of watercolour paper, usually combining more than one flower and entwined with leaves or other items such as the vintage teapot and tea cups I'd included in one of the tea roses prints. They took about an hour or so to finish, if I got them right and didn't have to start with a fresh sketch.

After finishing painting for the night, I wasn't tired and wandered through the cottage having a look around at all the nooks and crannies I hadn't yet explored, wondering if Fintry had left any other folders or things behind. But no, nothing of interest.

However, when I opened the wardrobe I remembered about the dressmaker's fabric. It really was too late to start cutting and piecing an artwork landscape quilt together, for that's what I planned to do with some of the fabric. That was a job for the morning, in the daylight, when I could lay all the pieces out and study the colours.

I closed the wardrobe doors, padded through to the lounge and peered out the back window. I hadn't even had a chance to look inside the garden shed. A stash of fuel was kept in a kitchen cupboard near the sink and there was plenty left before I needed to top it up from the bags that had been delivered earlier.

Still...maybe I could light one of the lamps and venture outside. The storm had eased and it wasn't actually snowing. There was nothing to stop me going out. Suddenly, it felt like a small and mischievous adventure — wrapping up and heading outside at this time of night. Besides, the shed roof was heavy with snow. I should brush it off in case the weight warped the roof. Now I had an excuse for putting my jacket and boots on, grabbing the floor brush and a lamp, and going outside.

The air was freezing cold. I zipped my jacket up and walked over to the shed. The entire garden was frozen with snow and frost, and everything was silent. No sound from anywhere, not even the sea, which was strangely calm.

Walking past the trees felt like a scene from an ethereal wonderland. Enchanting, I thought. Right now, it felt like the most enchanting garden I'd ever been in. I remembered my grandfather used to shake the snow from the branches of his pear and cherry trees to prevent the branches breaking from the extra weight or becoming misshapen. I shook the trees as I went past and knocked the snow off with the brush.

'You're full of surprises,' a man's voice said from nearby.

I gasped and spun around to see Tavion standing smiling at me.

'Oh, it's you. You scared me. What are you doing here?'

'No one had seen or heard from you all day. I couldn't settle and didn't want to phone because you'd think I was a complete prat for worrying about you. I wanted to see if the lights were on in your cottage. Then I'd know you were okay. I know you can take care of yourself, but in this weather, it's dangerous. Don't worry, I won't be making a habit of this. Clearly you're well capable of looking after yourself. Anyone spring cleaning the garden at this hour, in the snow, is a tiger in my book.'

'I suppose you'll be wanting a cuppa?'

'No, no I'm not coming in. As I say, I just wanted to check you were okay. Newcomers don't always know the way of things around here.'

'That's a shame. I'd baked scones earlier. I've some left. I'll toast them in the morning for breakfast.'

'Scones, huh?'

I nodded.

'You've twisted my arm,' he said.

‘Do you think I could twist it further?’ I held the brush out to him. ‘I’m not tall enough to brush the snow off the roof of the shed. Would you mind?’

‘For tea and a home baked scone I’ll even brush the boughs of the trees for you.’

‘I’ll put the kettle.’ I left him to deal with the shed roof and hurried inside.

We sat in the kitchen having tea and scones and chatted about the other cottages in the area.

‘Tell me about the beemaster’s cottage. Does he have any old–fashioned bee hives? I’d love to sketch and paint them when the weather is better.’

‘The beemaster has some fine hives, a lot of them are years old.’

‘Do you think he’d mind me painting them?’

‘I’m sure he’d be pleased, especially if you gave him one of your paintings.’

‘I’d definitely do that.’

‘I’ll mention it to him. He’s away this month. And I must bring you a jar of the beemaster’s honey. I’ve got a couple of jars at home. His cottage is next to my fields. His bees love my flowers, and of course the flowers in this cottage garden. The flavour of his honey varies from year to year depending on what flowers the bees frequent. I vary the flowers I grow, and you can taste the difference in the honey. He says that last year’s crop produced one of his favourite flavours. I’ll bring a jar next time for you.’

‘Thanks. It sounds tasty.’

‘If you’re on the Internet you can see his website with pictures of the bees and hives.’

‘I’ll do that.’

Tavion put his cup on the table and stood up. ‘I’ll be on my way. Thanks for the scones. They were delicious. There’s nothing to beat home baking.’

I stood at the kitchen door, arms wrapped across my chest to keep warm, and watched him walk away. He turned and waved. I waved back. I wasn’t sure what I felt about Tavion. A sense of down–to–earth trustworthiness. A fine looking man. Someone who wondered if I was okay when the entire world was getting ready to go to sleep. At the very least, he was a thoughtful new friend.

During the following two weeks I was more or less snowbound in the cottage, except when I visited Ethel. I made the most of it by finishing lots of my artwork — watercolours and acrylics, and sewing a landscape art quilt. I cut and pieced it together, using long strips of fabric. I based it on the local scenery, starting with shades of blue and grey for the sky. It was about the size of a large painting, and once it was finished I planned to hang it up as a wall art quilt. The main part was a seascape leading on to flowers and countryside. I included an appliqué of the cottage.

I hand stitched some of the quilt, and for other parts I used my sewing machine — and Ethel's machine. I popped in to see her every few days, trudging through the snow, and took my quilting with me. We shared tips on backing and binding the quilt. I used my gran's method of machine sewing the binding on to the front of the quilt and then finishing it by hand with slip stitches after folding the binding to the back.

Although I'd been quite prepared to spend a lot of time on my own living at the cottage, I enjoyed Ethel's company and we'd become good friends. She even taught me how to spin yarn properly, something I'd never considered learning. Her classes didn't start until February so she'd suggested I learn while it was quiet. Though there wasn't much quiet when we got together, chatting for hours. She knew all the gossip.

Whenever she brought up the subject of Fintry I felt guilty about keeping his whereabouts a secret. I didn't even tell her about the book proposal. Franklin was now in touch with Fintry by email and phone, discussing aspects of the book, leaving me free to get on with my own work. However, Franklin had mentioned that I would be paid and credited for additional artwork included.

Apart from two brief emails thanking me for putting him in contact with Franklin, I hadn't heard from Fintry, though he did tell me he was hoping to search for the new flower when the snow melted. According to the local forecast, the last of the snow would fall at the end of January, making way for a bright, early spring.

One morning at the start of February I woke up and most of the snow had gone. It had taken its toll on the garden, but it was heartening to see the first snowdrops pop up through the frosty ground, followed by crocus and daffodils.

I went for a brisk walk along the shore, sensing that the winter had finally given way to the spring. The sea air felt a bit milder. That was the day I started to tackle the garden, clearing the debris leftover from the winter months and preparing the ground for new plants. Old–fashioned four o'clocks were to be nurtured as a hedge along the front garden. According to the notes in the folder, these flowers opened late afternoon and produced a heady fragrance at night.

I lit the oil heater in the shed, wiped down the window inside and out to let in the daylight, and set to work using the tools that were hanging up in the shed. At first I was wary of using them in case I damaged them. One of the garden spades had a date carved into the wooden handle — 1952, but the shaft was sturdy and riveted to the steel. It weighed a ton, but it cut through the debris on the ground easier than any other shovel I'd used, allowing me to clear away the remnants of winter and turn the soil over. It looked rich and dark, and I couldn't wait to start planting new seedlings and nurturing the established plants, bringing everything back to thrive again. The peonies had withstood the fierce weather, and I was hopeful they would flower later in the spring and into the summer. They were hardy little souls, adept at taking care of themselves, thriving year after year. Something I aimed to do.

I cleaned the tools after use, hung them back up and realised I'd worked right through lunch. Only now in the afternoon did the hunger hit me.

'The garden's looking great,' Tavion called to me as he was going by.

I smiled and waved over.

'I'm going down to the shops at the harbour. Do you need anything?'

I'd gone to the shops early in the morning for fresh milk and bread, so I didn't need groceries. And the fortnightly supply of shopping had continued to be delivered. But there was something he could do for me.

'Hang on.' I ran inside and grabbed the latest letter I'd written to my gran. I hurried out to him. 'Could you post this letter for me? I've put a stamp on it.'

Tavion took the letter and put it in his jacket pocket. 'Happy to do that for you. Sure you don't need anything else?'

'No, I'm fine, thanks.'

'I keep forgetting to bring you that jar of honey I promised. If I remember, I'll drop it off later, after dinner.'

'Sorry. It's Ethel's birthday. She's having a yarn party at her house this evening. A girls' night — knitting, drinking and having a giggle.'

He nodded thoughtfully and then said, 'Will Glen be there?'

'She was supposed to be coming, but she cancelled yesterday. She's too busy with her studies.'

I saw a flicker of hope and then disappointment in his eyes. 'Tell Ethel happy birthday from me.'

'I will do. And thanks for posting my letter.'

He walked away and I sensed a heaviness in his heart. If he still harboured hopes of getting together with Glen, I agreed with Ethel — from everything she'd told me about Glen and her ambitions, Tavion wasn't the man for her.

I wore my boots, a long brown corduroy skirt and a copper coloured jumper. I put my coat on and walked along to Ethel's cottage. Patches of crocus had fought their way through the grass, adding flashes of lilac, white, purple and yellow in the fading light. The evenings were starting to get a little brighter, especially on brisk evenings like this.

I'd wrapped her birthday present in flowery print paper, which seemed appropriate for the gift I'd made for her. For the past week I'd wondered what to buy her, then I decided to give her a painting of her cottage. I painted it in acrylics on a stretched canvas ready to hang. I'd asked to see photographs of her cottage, summer pictures, pretending I wanted to compare her garden flowers to those belonging to Fintry, but I really wanted to see what her cottage looked like during a summer's day. And that's what I painted — her lovely blue cottage with flowers, including delphiniums, sweet rocket and lilac.

Ethel told me she was baking a birthday cake, but all the ladies, around seven of us, promised to bring cake of some sort to share. I'd baked a strawberry and cream cake with luscious frosting, and an apple pie with shortcrust pastry. My gran loved to bake, and it was at times like this I realised how much I'd learned from her, even if sometimes my job was to peel and core the cooking apples for the pies. It was also my job to climb the apple trees in my grandparents' garden and pick the ripe fruit, the apples that were tart yet sweet, green with a rosy blush. When I was a girl, they tasted like the most delicious apples in the world. Still did.

I approached Ethel's cottage and was welcomed in.

'My goodness, you're loaded with everything,' Ethel exclaimed.

I put my bags down in the hallway. The bottle of whisky and bottle of sherry I'd brought with me clinked, giving away their contents. I handed the bag to Ethel. 'Cheers.'

She laughed. 'Now I wonder what's in this bag, eh?'

We went through to the lounge where the other women were seated. I wasn't late. They'd turned up early. Numerous gifts sat on the fireside table including a hand–knitted blue and white poncho and a long pair of yellow and brown stripe arm warmers.

Ethel put the poncho on. 'I've always wanted a poncho. Never got round to knitting one. I've tended to wear shawls, but this is very nice. Thank you, Hilda.'

I'd met the other ladies, at least once, during the times I was at Ethel's house or at the shops.

'It's blue and white, like the colours of your cottage,' said Hilda. 'I heard you mention you wanted to knit a poncho, so I thought this would suit you.'

Ethel smiled and then picked up the arm warmers.

A woman, in her late twenties, smiled back. 'I knitted the edges in bee stitch. They've got a lot of stretch in them. They'll keep your wrists and arms cosy while you're spinning the yarn.'

Other gifts were admired and enjoyed, and we all had a glass of whisky and sherry to toast Ethel's birthday.

I handed her the painting. 'And this is from me. Happy birthday, Ethel.'

She unwrapped it and then became quiet as she gazed at the painting.

For a moment I thought I'd done something wrong. But no.

She looked at me, blinking away tears as she smiled. 'This is beautiful, Mairead.'

The others gathered round, and then I helped Ethel hang it up where she could admire it while she was working.

As we shared out the cakes with equal amounts of gossip and laughter, I felt like I belonged there, part of their community. They'd never made me feel like an outsider.

Ethel squeezed my hand. 'Are you okay?'

'Just thinking about things.' I smiled. 'I don't mean to appear melancholy because I'm not. I'm happy to be here.' Too happy. That was the problem. With each week that passed I loved living there more and more. How would I ever leave?

'Missing home?' Ethel whispered.

'No, the complete opposite, though I do miss my grandparents, but we're in touch so regularly that I feel they're part of everything I'm doing.'

'There's a cottage near here that's going to be available for rent,' said Ethel.

'That's the one down by the harbour,' said Hilda, overhearing us.

'Yes,' said Ethel. 'Tavion told me recently that the woman who lives there is retiring and going to live with her family abroad for a year, so she's renting out the cottage.'

They all looked at me. I didn't know what to say.

'Something to think about, Mairead,' said Ethel. 'Plenty of time to consider it. Who knows, maybe you'll be here celebrating my next birthday with me.'

Would I? Could I move here permanently when Fintry came back to the cottage? The thoughts swirled around in my mind.

'Can I top up your glass with a wee bitty more whisky?' Ethel stood beside me, poised with the bottle ready to pour.

I went to put my hand over my glass then I reconsidered. 'Thanks, I think I could do with it.' I wasn't one for having a drink, so two glasses of a very potent whisky made me quite tipsy.

'Tavion says to wish you happy birthday, Ethel,' I remembered to tell her.

'You seem to be getting quite friendly with him,' she said, winking at the others.

'We're just friends,' I insisted. 'No more. He even asked if Glen was going to be here at the party. That was the first thing he asked me. He looked disappointed when I said she wouldn't be here.'

'Glen's not his type,' one of the ladies remarked. 'She's too much of a firecracker. A talented young woman who'll go far.'

Hilda agreed. 'Tavion needs someone who is happy to settle down here.' She looked at me. 'Someone like you, Mairead.'

'No, Tavion isn't...we're not...I mean.'

Hilda smiled knowingly at the other ladies, and then said to me, 'Unless you've got your eye on someone else.'

'I don't have my eye on anyone,' I said. 'I'm too busy with my work.'

'Not even the flower hunter?' Hilda suggested.

'I hardly know Fintry.'

'He's the type of man a woman could meet and fall in lust with first go,' one of the ladies remarked.

Hilda sighed. 'If I was forty years younger I'd be chasing Fintry round that garden of his never mind pruning it.'

'Anyone want a slice of Mairead's apple pie?' Ethel offered, bringing the matchmaking chat to a tactful end.

After eating the apple pie and sipping another round of whisky and sherry, the ladies conversation went back again to Fintry, and more home truths were shared.

CHAPTER SEVEN

Delphiniums

'Remember that young woman Fintry dated a couple of years ago?' said Hilda. 'Whatever happened to her?'

'She went back down to London,' said Ethel. 'She worked there, something to do with botanical work. That's how she met Fintry. By all accounts, she was the one doing all the running and followed him up to Scotland. It was never a serious relationship, not on his part. You could tell by the way he looked at her.'

'So their relationship fizzled out?' I asked.

Ethel nodded. 'I don't think Fintry's been involved with a girl since then. Far too busy with his work. From what I've heard, his father wants him to settle down. By the time all the men in that family were in their late twenties they were married.'

'Maybe he's not the marrying kind,' I suggested.

The ladies laughed.

'Oh I think he is,' said Ethel. 'At our New Year céilidh, he got a wee bit tipsy and told me he wished he could find the woman for him. Of course, the following day he said it was the whisky talking, but I think he's a romantic at heart.' She glanced at me. 'Perhaps you'll fall for Fintry.'

'There's little chance of that. By the time he gets back to the cottage I'll be leaving.'

'Well, never mind,' said Ethel. 'There are a few eligible men around these parts.'

'The chocolatier,' said Hilda.

'And the beemaster,' Ethel added.

One of the ladies giggled. 'I've a wee crush on the beemaster. He's too young for me, about the same age as Fintry and the chocolatier, early thirties. And my husband wouldn't be happy, but I bet his kisses taste as sweet as his honey.'

'I haven't met him,' I said. 'Tavion said he's away on business.'

'I'll introduce you when he gets back,' Ethel promised. 'He's a treat to see on a summer's day with his shirt off, tending to his garden or striding along the shore and diving into the sea.'

The others murmured in agreement.

I laughed.

'Not that we spend all our time talking about men and ogling the local totty,' said Ethel.

'Just a lot of your time,' I teased them.

Ethel grinned. 'And is there anything wrong with that?'

I held up my hands. 'Not a thing.'

Ethel stood up. 'Right, I'm lighting my birthday cake candles again and having another round of wishes. Anyone want to share in a wish?'

I'd never heard of such a thing. Sharing birthday wishes?

Ethel stuck candles in individual slices of cake and handed them round to everyone. She used a long match from the fireplace to light them. I went along with everything they did. I closed my eyes, blew out the candle on my piece of cake and made a wish. I wished that I would find romance and happiness here.

As we blew out our candles the lights in the cottage flickered and dimmed for a second. We screamed, giggled and gasped. Tavion would've called it a 'brown out' but the ladies took it to be a portent that some of our wishes would come true.

We sat and chatted for another hour or so, exchanging stories, hopes and dreams.

Ethel cupped a glass of whisky in her hands and watched the amber liquid shine with the light from the fire. 'I worry about Glen,' she confided. 'Not about her career, but for her happiness. I worry that her ambition will stop her finding contentment.'

The others nodded.

Ethel continued, 'She's dating a musician, but even she admits it's just a wee fling. When she looks back, is she going to see a load of accolades and little more than that?'

'It's a difficult one,' said Hilda. 'Glen's talented and her fashion work is going to take her all over the world to fashion shows in London, Paris, Milan and New York.'

'I know,' said Ethel. 'And I'll never try to curtail her. I just wish...' She sighed and looked at me. 'You're talented, Mairead, but you seem to want romance in your life.'

'All the women here tonight are talented,' I said. 'You spin and sell your yarn, Ethel. Hilda makes and sells quilts. There are those who knit, sew or bake for a living, running their businesses from home. That takes hard work and talent, but most of you are or were married, so maybe Glen will relax more when she comes here to learn to spin the yarn for her textile designs.'

'Yes, you're right,' Ethel said to me. She glanced at her glass of whisky. 'I've probably had one too many of these. Drink makes me maudlin. I'm going to put the kettle on for a cuppa.'

'Perhaps Glen will get married,' said Hilda. 'The dressmaker said that a young woman, an outsider, who comes to live here, will have an offer of marriage this summer.'

Ethel's eyes lit up with realisation. 'We all assumed it would be Glen.' She flicked a glance at me. 'What if it's not Glen? What if it's you, Mairead?'

'An offer of marriage? I don't think so.'

One of the ladies nudged me. 'Maybe Tavion will ask you to marry him. Wouldn't that be exciting?'

I shook my head and laughed. 'I'll help you put the kettle on, Ethel. I think we all need to sober up and have a cuppa.'

But deep inside, while I set the teacups on the trays, I wondered about the dressmaker's prediction.

'Is the dressmaker usually accurate when it comes to things like this?' I asked Ethel.

'She rarely passes messages to us, but she told the woman who works for her to tell us this at New Year. It depends on how you interpret things I suppose, but she's always accurate.' She topped up the milk jug. 'Even if you're not into all that sort of fey stuff, she really is a fantastic dressmaker. I hope when Glen is here she'll be invited up to her house to learn her sewing skills. It has to be by special invitation. She passes her skills on to very, very few.'

Ethel and I carried the trays through.

While the chatter circled around me, I gazed out the window at the sea, far in the distance, so dark and wild. An offer of marriage? I doubted it.

'Here's Tavion,' said Hilda. 'He's got a bunch of flowers for you, Ethel.'

Ethel hurried through to let him in.

'I know it's a girls' night only, but I couldn't let your birthday go by without giving you something,' I heard him say.

'Come in. The girls have been having a wee tipple. Don't worry, they won't ravish you.'

'My plan has been foiled yet again.' He followed her through, carrying a bunch of flowers and a box of chocolates. 'Happy birthday, Ethel.' He gave her a kiss on the cheek, causing the women to cheer.

'I got a kiss on my birthday from a handsome man after all. One wish came true.'

'We were just talking about you,' one of the ladies told him.

'No wonder my ears were burning.'

'Yes,' she said, her cheeks bright with one sherry over her limit. 'We were marrying you off to Glen or Mairead.'

He gave me a broad smile.

'Ssh!' Ethel scolded her, then said to Tavion, 'We were talking nonsense.'

Tavion was still smiling. 'I certainly approve of your choices for me, though I've no plans yet to find myself a wife.' He glanced at a framed photograph of Glen on the mantelpiece. She was willowy with glossy auburn hair, a pale complexion, and wore one of the dresses she'd designed and modelled for a fashion show. Glen was beautiful.

Ethel invited Tavion to join us and have a slice of birthday cake.

'No, I just dropped by to give you a pressie, Ethel. It's getting late anyway.'

Ethel wrapped a piece of cake in a napkin and he put it in his pocket. 'I've included a wee candle. Have a wish on me.'

'I'll do that.' He seemed to know they did this.

Two of the women decided to leave with him.

'Wait for us,' said Hilda. 'We'll walk along with you.'

While they got their coats on he remembered he had a message for Ethel.

'The postmaster says to tell you to drop by. He's got a birthday present for you.'

Ethel's face lit up. 'Oooh! I wonder what it is.'

Tavion didn't know. 'I offered to bring it here, but he wants to give you a little something personally.'

Hilda wrapped her silk scarf around her neck. 'I bet he does.' Her tone was laced with innuendo.

The women laughed.

'Is there something going on between you and the postmaster, Ethel?' I asked her.

'Not for a long time. Certainly not these days.' Ethel gave me a cheeky grin. 'We've had our moments in the past.'

'Quite a few of them if I recall correctly,' said Hilda.

Ethel's eyes had a distant look. 'I used to be quite pretty.'

'She was a stoater,' said Hilda. 'You think Glen's beautiful? Huh, you should've seen Ethel.'

Ethel smiled at her friend and gave her a hug as she left with Tavion. He had one woman on each arm.

'Oh, I can feel your muscles,' Hilda chirped as they walked away.

The rest of them started to get our coats and jackets on to leave. I was the last to go because I offered to help Ethel tidy up the dishes.

I dried the plates and put them in the cupboard.

'Thanks for helping me, Mairead. You're a wee gem.'

I gave a quick tidy to the living room and put the folding chairs she used for her classes back beside the spinning wheels.

'I have to thank you again for the painting. I love it.'

I put my coat on and wrapped my scarf around the collar. 'I'm glad you like it.'

She waved me off at the door.

I walked along the coastal path, admiring the sea. And I wondered about Fintry. Would I ever get a chance to sail on his yacht? I'd never been sailing. I imagined what it would be like to drift across the water on sunny days or evenings. Fanciful thoughts.

I saw the flower hunter's cottage in the distance. It felt like home, but it wasn't my home and never would be. For now, I was living a temporary life. Franklin had given me something to think about when I'd emailed artwork to him that morning for approval. He emailed back.

Love the artwork, especially the Cupid's darts, delphiniums, sweet peas, and four o'clocks. You're well ahead of the book deadline. Keep up the great work. When the lease is finished on the flower hunter's cottage, consider moving down here to London. Daisy, who used to be my main botanical illustrator, is living permanently in Cornwall. She's not coming back to London. You could work for me at the publishers. Just something to think about. All the best, Franklin.

The following days consisted of work. I was gradually getting the garden tamed and had potted seedlings ready for planting. I enjoyed working in the garden. All the fresh air and outdoor living started to put some colour in my cheeks. As the time went on I felt more settled — working during the day and sewing my quilts or preparing other artwork in the evenings. I hardly watched television unless one of my favourite films was on.

I visited Ethel often and she let me try the new spinning wheel the postmaster had given her as a gift. When I say new, it was actually a vintage wheel in full working order.

'The postmaster thought it would give me an extra one for teaching the spinning,' she told me.

And so, with everything feeling content, Fintry's email came as quite a jolt.

Mairead. Franklin has suggested I contact you. I'm still searching for the new flower. No joy yet. When I mentioned this to Franklin, he said it would be great if you could sketch an illustration, from real life, when I find it, and we'll include it in my book with the other flower hunting work. A sort of conclusion to the book. What do you think? Could you come up to my house for a couple of days and go with me on my next exped? I hope so. You will of course be paid for your time and work. Let me know what you think.

What did I think? First thought...go flower hunting? Yes, definitely. How exciting. Then common sense kicked in. Stay with Fintry at his house? Keep all of this a secret from everyone, including Ethel? No mean feat. I decided to sleep on my reply and email him in the morning.

Before breakfast, I made my decision.

Okay, I'll go. When were you planning on leaving? What do I need to bring with me?

The whole idea unnerved me slightly. I wasn't sure why. Was it because I'd have to make up plausible excuses for where I was going to Ethel and Tavion? They'd worry if I suddenly disappeared for a couple of days without telling them. Or was it the thought of being with Fintry?

I made porridge for breakfast, shivering while the stove started to warm up the kitchen. I wore cosy leggings and a thick jumper. A layer of frost sparkled across the garden. Spring was here but the February mornings were still brisk. I ate my bowl of porridge and milk, gazing out the kitchen window and waiting for Fintry's reply.

It arrived as I was washing up the dishes.

That's great, Mairead. Could you come up here this evening? I know it's short notice, and it's fine if you can't. I'm planning to set off very early tomorrow morning. Bring warm, comfortable clothing. Walking boots if you have them, or similar. Basically, items to keep you warm and dry. Layers are ideal. I have thermals you can borrow and a backpack if you need it for your artwork.

I typed my reply.

I'll drive up this evening. Give me directions. I don't think you're too far away.

No, not far. He gave a link to the directions on a map. It seemed straightforward. *I'll meet you at the halfway point at nine o'clock. Phone if you get lost. I'll come and get you. And I don't think I have to remind you not to tell anyone where I am and what we'll be getting up to.*

Getting up to? Why did that set my heart pounding? This wasn't a romantic clandestine liaison. This was business. Work. Art. Nothing more than traipsing through the countryside with an extremely handsome man. Think of it as an adventure, I told myself. Part of the whole experience of living at the cottage. I was free to do what I wanted, and tonight I'd be heading off to meet Fintry, kitted out with sensible clothing.

And that's exactly what I did. Well...perhaps not exactly. A pretty top and non sensible skirt made the final cut into my suitcase when I was packing.

I left word with Ethel and Tavion that I was going to an art convention and would be away for a couple of days. It was a little white lie, but I couldn't tell them about Fintry. I was going to be working on my art so it wasn't that far from the truth.

I drove along the narrow road with my headlights at full beam. Trees arched over the road and I couldn't see anything except hedgerows and fields.

A car flashed its headlights at me further along the road. Fintry was waiting to meet me as promised. My heart gave a little leap of joy and relief.

I pulled up beside his car. He got out and came over to me, that handsome face of his smiling. He looked genuinely pleased to see me.

'My house is about a mile from here, but the roads are narrow and twisty and it's difficult to find.'

'I'll follow you,' I said to him through my car window.

He gave me the thumbs up and ran back to his car.

We set off in tandem and I kept up as my car navigated the road which at some parts was little more than a dirt track.

We reached the two–storey farmhouse where he was staying and parked in the driveway.

'I'll help you in with your bags,' he said, lifting all four of them at once.

Don't think about how fit and strong he is, I scolded myself. I loved a man who looked good in classy cords and a jumper. The neutral creams and caramel tones of his clothes suited his burnished blond hair.

We went inside. He flicked the lights on in the lounge and kitchen.

'Make yourself at home, Mairead. I'll get the fire going. Your bedroom is through here.'

He led the way, carrying my bags. He put them down on the bedroom floor. Two bedside lamps gave a glow to the room which was traditionally furnished with lots of chintz, as was the lounge.

'This is lovely.'

'I'm on the other side of the house, so you'll have plenty of privacy.'

He towered over me in the bedroom and for a moment I thought I saw a hint of interest in his eyes.

'I'll make us something to eat. Come through when you're ready.'

I unpacked my things, freshened up in the en suite bathroom and gazed at my nervous reflection in the mirror. Calm down. Don't act like a fool.

I went through to the lounge. He'd lit the fire, and unless he was the fussy type, he'd also tidied the lounge before coming to meet me. The cushions on the sofa and chairs were just so. The rugs on the wooden floor were hoovered. Nothing lying around. I was flattered he'd bothered to make it look nice.

The kitchen was just off the lounge and I saw Fintry dashing around cooking. What on earth was he making? It looked like he'd already prepared a full dinner and was attempting to heat it up before serving.

'Do you want a hand?' I sensed something was in danger of burning on the stove. A stew by the aroma wafting through.

'Two hands. I think I've misjudged the roast potatoes.'

Roast potatoes?

He opened the oven door and bent down to inspect them. 'Do these look ready to you?' He grabbed an oven glove and pulled the tray out to show me.

The potatoes sizzled in olive oil, all crispy and golden.

'Yes, they're ready. I didn't expect you to go to all this bother.' I stirred the stew in the pot. 'This looks ready too. Do you want me to start serving it up while you make the tea?' He'd set dinner plates on the kitchen table and gingham napkins.

'Deal.' He sounded relieved and set about filling the teapot with boiling water.

I spooned the stew, which had plenty of vegetables along with the meat and gravy, on to our plates. Then I divided the roast potatoes between us.

'There's sea salt in the cupboard if you want it.'

I did. I sprinkled it over my roasties.

He sat down and did the same.

He smiled across the table at me. 'I can't quite believe you're here. When Franklin suggested I ask you, I thought you'd say no.'

I frowned. 'Why?'

He shrugged his broad shoulders. Only now did I notice he wore a shirt under his creamy knit jumper. Very stylish, and far too attractive for his own good.

'You're busy with your own work at the cottage. It was short notice, and it's quite a task to go out into the hills hunting for flowers in this weather. I was up one of the mountainside paths yesterday and I couldn't see the top for the low–hanging mist. The day warmed up later on, but given the choice of sitting at home in the cottage beside a cosy fire painting flowers or taking on the elements to paint outdoors, I know what option I'd choose.'

'Outdoors, challenging the elements, and yourself.'

He laughed, and stabbed a fork into one of his roasties. 'Franklin said you've got a great nature, easy going.' He smiled over at me. 'I'm glad you're here.'

'So am I. I'm looking forward to seeing how a flower hunter actually hunts.'

'Lots of walking, more walking, searching through the undergrowth, avoiding the rain and freezing conditions, more walking and hoping to find an elusive flower. A one in a million shot.'

'The odds are that good, eh?'

'Better than I'd bet for you being here with me.'

He grinned, causing the dimples in his cheeks to form and triggered all sorts of reactions within me.

'I really do want to thank you for putting me in contact with Franklin.'

'You're welcome. When I saw the folders with all those wonderful notes and drawings, I thought — this is a book that Franklin would publish. His company publish gorgeous non–fiction books. Most are heavily illustrated. And he's such a lovely person to work with.'

'He said the same about you.'

'That was nice of him.' I paused and then told him about the job offer. 'He's offered me the chance to work with him in London once I've finished the lease at your cottage.'

'London? So you'd move away?' It was the first time I'd seen him frown.

'Well, yes. After all, I am a city girl. I think I could fit in living and working there.'

'Wouldn't you miss the rural life? The cottage? Fresh sea air?'

'Of course, but you'll have moved back by then and I have no other options in the pipeline. Franklin says I should think it over. It's an excellent offer, and it might not be forever. I could work in London until I figure out where I belong.'

He toyed with his food and didn't look up. 'Maybe you'll come back one day?'

'Maybe I will.'

He was quiet for a moment, and then he said, 'How are you getting on with Tavion?'

'Fine. He helped me brush snow off the roof of your shed in exchange for a home baked scone. I wasn't tall enough to reach without climbing up a frosty ladder.'

He tried to smile. 'Sounds as if you two have become quite friendly.'

'Yes, you have very friendly neighbours.' I told him about Ethel's birthday party, including Tavion turning up with gifts and leaving with a woman on each arm.

'Perhaps I'm in the wrong business. I should be a flower grower rather than a hunter. Tavion seems to be having all the fun.'

'One of the ladies was Hilda so nothing scandalous went on.' I kept my tone light–hearted. I could sense he was slightly envious of his so–called friendly rival.

'Tavion has always been the most popular with the ladies. I must try harder.'

'Nonsense. You're far more gorgeous than him.' The words were out before I could stop myself. I blushed and started to clear the dishes away, hurrying through to the kitchen to wash them.

I was aware of Fintry standing at my shoulder moments later. I didn't look round as he murmured, 'Thank you, Mairead.'

I kept washing the plates and cutlery in the soapy water. 'Pay no attention to my ramblings. I'm overtired. It's been one of those days.'

'That's a pity because I quite liked the notion of going to sleep thinking that you thought I was gorgeous.'

I turned around to find him smiling at me, trying not to laugh at me squirming with embarrassment. 'You're not that gorgeous. In fact, when you're wearing that cocky grin, you're about a two on the scale of gorgeousness.'

'Is there such a scale?'

'There might be.'

He laughed. 'You're really cute when you blush.'

'I'm not blushing. It's rage.'

He pressed his oh so kissable lips together. 'Well, you look cute when you're angry too.' And then he smirked.

I grabbed the tea towel and tried to swipe him with it. He dodged it like a pro.

I flicked it at him again and again. All he did was sidestep and laugh even more.

I cast the cloth aside.

'Throwing in the tea towel, Mairead?'

I sighed at the way he kept teasing me. 'Okay. I give up.'

He stepped closer.

'I never give up going after something elusive, something I know may not be attainable, when I want it.' There was an element of romance in his voice mixed with a hunter's instinct that sent pleasurable shivers through me.

CHAPTER EIGHT

Love–in–a–Mist

After dinner, Fintry stretched his long legs out by the fireside while I curled up on the sofa.

He had a map of where we were heading and laid it out on the coffee table.

'This is the valley we're tackling tomorrow. It's about an hour's drive if the weather stays calm.'

The weather was probably a lot calmer than the beating of my heart, seeing him near me. The contours of his features were highlighted by the glow of the fire, and I had the most aching urge to hug him. I'd never felt like that before. Yes, I'd met plenty of attractive men, but there was something about Fintry that made my senses yearn to be near him. Yearn for something I knew I could never have. A man like him could have his pick of beautiful women. I was interesting rather than beautiful. Pretty enough on a good day. Slim, bordering on a bit on the scrawny side. Even a full dinner with stew and roast potatoes, or the wholesome meals I was eating at the cottage, wouldn't put much meat on my bones. I felt like a livewire most times, as if I was burning energy either through excitement, hard work, physical work in the garden every day, and then work of some sort in the evenings. Perpetual motion, never still. I needed to learn to be still, like Ethel, even like Tavion. That, I supposed, would take time. And now I was about to charge off into the Highlands with Fintry. No rest for the wicked or botanical artists who chose to go off on spur of the moment adventures.

'We've got an early start.' Fintry stood up and stretched, giving me quite a view of his fit physique. 'We'd better get to bed.'

I guffawed. I knew what he meant but couldn't help sniggering, especially when his face burned with embarrassment.

'Separate beds. That's what a meant.'

I was still smirking as I walked to my bedroom. 'Goodnight, Fintry. See you in the morning.'

'I've set an alarm for six.'

'See you in a few hours then.'

I heard him laugh as we went our separate ways to grab some sleep. It was after one in the morning. We'd lost all measure of time, sitting chatting by the fire after scoffing dinner and following through with a glass of wine.

The bed looked very inviting — one of those beds with plumped up pillows and an eiderdown that you could disappear into for a week. Far too comfy when I only had a handful of hours sleep time before our early start.

After rummaging through all four bags, I realised I was miles away from my pyjamas. Off all the things to forget to pack. Never mind, I thought, and jumped into bed starkers. The room was warm and I was so tired I fell asleep within minutes.

I awoke with a scream, feeling something warm and hairy brush along the length of my thigh. Disoriented in the dark, forgetting for a moment where I was, I yelled out again.

Fintry came running to my rescue and flicked on the bedside lights. I'd no idea where the switch was.

'What's wrong, Mairead? Were you having a bad dream?'

I clutched the quilt to cover my nakedness. 'Something touched my thigh. Something — alive.'

'It wasn't me.'

'I felt something was prowling around my bed.'

Fintry spread his arms out and glanced around the room. 'There's nothing here.' He stepped closer. 'You're shaking.'

'I could've sworn something touched me.' I hated sounding jittery. Then there was the fact that Fintry was wearing a pair of tight–fitting white pants that left nothing, and I mean *nothing*, to the imagination. Jeez–oh.

'Would you like me to make you a cup of hot milk?'

At the mention of milk, a scratching noise sounded from underneath the bed.

I jumped out of bed and dived on Fintry, wrapping myself around him and clinging on. Not in a lustful way, but in a save me from whatever monster is lurking under there sort of way.

He held me close which had two benefits and one huge disadvantage. The benefits were, my feet were off the floor so whatever was scuffling around couldn't bite me, and with my body pressed against his he couldn't see my nakedness. He could feel me though, and I could feel his bare chest against mine and strong shoulders that my fingers refused to let go of. The latter was the disadvantage. OMG! How had I ended up in this compromising position? It was going to take more than a cup of hot milk to calm me down.

Unperturbed, he carried me through to the lounge, sat me down on the sofa and put a throw around me while averting his gaze.

Please tell me he wasn't used to behaviour like this. Let him just be calm and commanding.

'Wait here. I think I know who it is.' He went through to the bedroom and came back carrying a large white cat. It purred as he patted its head. 'Mystery solved. It was Snowdrop.'

'You should've told me you had a cat.'

'I forgot.'

'You forgot you had a cat?'

'It's not my cat. Remember, this isn't my house. It belongs to friends who are away on holiday.'

It was obvious the cat liked him, and was content to be lifted up and fussed over.

'We'd better get you a saucer of milk,' he said, causing the cat to meow.

While he was busy in the kitchen, I cast the throw aside and made a bolt for it through to my room and jumped into bed.

After feeding the cat, Fintry wandered through to check on me. 'Do you want me to flick the lights off?'

'Yes, and thanks for coming to my rescue even if it was only the cat.'

'No problem.' He tried not to smile. 'I eh, I didn't see anything.'

I looked at him. That was a blatant lie.

'Okay, so I saw everything, but only for a moment,' he admitted. 'You're very fast on your feet. Your eh, your...everything was a bit of a blur.'

Like hell is was. I smiled anyway, wishing he'd put the lights out.

'Goodnight, Mairead. Snowdrop is in his basket. He won't bother you again tonight.' He flicked the lights off, but his physique was silhouetted in the doorway from the light shining through from the lounge. What a build. He had a set of abdominals like a competitive swimmer and a lean, hard torso to die for.

I fluffed my pillows and tried to settle down, trying not to think that I had been right earlier — Fintry was gorgeous.

I woke before the alarm having had a restless night. After a quick shower, I put on warm, sensible clothes suitable for trekking into the wilds.

Fintry knocked on the bedroom door. 'Are you decent?'

'Yes.' Unlike last night. 'You can come in.'

'Breakfast's almost ready.' When he opened the door the smell of toast wafted in.

I followed him through to the kitchen, passing Snowdrop in the lounge who was sound asleep in his basket.

'We'll let him sleep,' said Fintry. 'I've left him plenty to eat and drink, and he lets himself in and out via the cat door.'

Sausages, potato scones and tomatoes were browning under the grill.

'Grab a plate and help yourself,' he said.

So I did. We sat together at the kitchen table.

'I've planned the route we'll take. Mist is forecast on higher ground, but we're not climbing today.'

'Climbing?' Apple trees and the occasional ladder were my limit.

'Not mountaineering,' he assured me. 'Think of it as hillwalking at a steep angle.'

'Climbing?' I repeated.

'Sort of, but without the need for ropes or crampons. More scrambling, but I'll be doing most of that while you draw the scenery.'

He motioned towards two rucksacks. I hoped the small one was mine.

'I've packed some things we'll need. Your rucksack has plenty of room left for your artwork materials, camera and whatever else you need. I'll carry extra fleece tops and waterproofs for us in case the weather changes. It's forecast to be a grey, brisk day, comfortable for where we're heading.'

'I'm assuming you know the area well.' I suddenly wanted reassurance. I had no sense of direction. And clearly no sense at all considering I was basically going hiking at an angle so steep it was borderline climbing.

He finished eating his potato scone and shook his head. 'No, never been to this area. It'll be an adventure for both of us.'

Maybe it was the colour draining from my face that made him stop winding me up.

'Yes, of course I know this area. I've been living round these parts since I was a boy.'

I glared at him and then at a tea towel near the stove.

He got up and threw it over the overhead pulley out of my reach. He gave me a mischievous smile. 'You'll have to climb up to get it, and I don't think climbing is your thing.'

'Don't bet on it.'

'I rarely bet on anything, especially when it comes to beautiful women.'

'Flattery won't save you from a tea towel whipping.'

'Worth a shot though, eh?'

We laughed and continued teasing each other while clearing the breakfast things away.

Fintry loaded the rucksacks and a picnic basket into the car and we set off for the hidden valley.

'Picnic?' I said, looking at the grey sky that stretched for miles around us. 'It's not exactly picnic weather.'

'I live in hope,' he said, throwing me a sexy grin. 'I always live in hope.'

Through rough trails and dense forest, we drove deeper into the depths of the valley. The grey sky darkened across the landscape as we neared the parking point. Hills covered in patches of purple and white heather, bracken and gorse, shielded us from the outside world. No one else was around for miles. We hadn't even driven past anyone on the last part of the route.

I got out of the car to stretch my legs and gazed up at the sky. I felt tiny. A dot on this magnificent landscape. The wild and rugged beauty was breathtaking. I took some photographs knowing they wouldn't do justice to the awe–inspiring sights around me.

Fintry pointed to one of the mid–range hills. It was scattered with hardy spring heather, thick patches of trees and sheer rock, like slate, as if someone had scraped it to the bone. 'We're heading over there. It'll take us a while. It's a fair walk. Let me know at any time if you get tired.' He patted one side of his rucksack. 'I've got a flask of tea.

There's nothing to beat a cuppa and sandwiches outdoors in weather like this.'

I glanced at the picnic basket on the back seat of the car.

'That's for when we get back.' He reached over and opened it up. A small bottle of champagne was inside along with the food. 'In case we get lucky and have something to celebrate.'

We set off and chatted as we walked. I asked him about his flower hunting.

'How do you know there's a new species near here?'

'I don't. Hillwalkers were here before the winter set in. They posted photographs online. Someone noticed the flowers in the pictures and word got round that it was maybe a new species. I heard about it, and here we are. I've already scoured the area for the past couple of weeks, and unfortunately there's no hint of anything special. I've even climbed to the top ridges. This is probably the last weekend I'll search for it. I'm pleased you could be here.'

'So it's a long shot that you'll find it, and even if you do, it could be a known plant?'

'Yes. A lot of hunting is research work, searching for information and being prepared to travel wherever necessary in the hope of finding an undiscovered gem.'

'And you're a man who lives in hope.'

'Indeed I am.'

After an hour we stopped near the top of one of the hills and had a short break.

Fintry poured two cups of tea from his flask and gave me a choice of sandwiches — cheese and pickle or chicken and salad. We ended up sharing a bit of both.

We sat together gazing out over some of the most beautiful scenery I'd ever seen. Far in the distance I saw a long, silvery sheen cutting through the mountain ridges. A river. This is how I'd paint it. A streak of silver beneath the vast grey sky and surrounded by mountains in every shade of magenta and violet my artist's palette could create.

'It's so quiet,' I murmured.

'I come here once a year if I can. When the world becomes too noisy, I like to breath in the quiet. Sometimes it's busier in the summer months, but I've hardly ever met anyone when I've been here.' He glanced at me. 'It's nice to have your company. Someone who appreciates the grand quietude and has an artist's eye for the all the colours in the hills and the sky.' He looked out across the land. 'I've never actually had a conversation here.'

'I can be quiet.'

'No, I like to hear you talk. It's calming.'

I laughed. 'Even my grandparents who have tons of patience say I'm a chatterbox.'

'Maybe they just don't hear you the way I do.' He smiled at me. 'Don't ever change how you are, Mairead. Not for anyone.'

The wind blew through his tousled blond hair. Without thinking, I reached over and brushed a couple of wayward strands away from his eyes. Realising what I'd done, I pulled my hand back, but he clasped hold of my hand and held it in his. He kissed my hand and then let it go.

Not a word was exchanged for several minutes as we sat together side by side. Not a word was needed.

Fintry finally packed the flask in his rucksack and we were on our way again, exploring the hills and valley for the elusive flower. I wanted him to find it, and yet in my heart it didn't matter. I think that day, all alone together, miles from home, we both found a deeper friendship. We were friends with potential. And like Fintry, I started to live in hope.

While he climbed up a particularly steep slope, I sat down and painted a couple of rough sketches using my small watercolour box. It was great for painting outdoors. I'd selected a set of little half pans in assorted colours that I thought I would need — Prussian blue, ultramarine, gamboge, burnt umber, alizarin crimson, sap, cobalt violet and a few others.

I tried not to worry about how high up he was as he appeared to be well experienced, agile and strong, but not headstrong. He didn't take any unnecessary risks to show–off to me. If anything, he was an assured mountaineer.

I painted him into one of the pictures, intending to add more details later.

By late afternoon the weather darkened and we began to head back to the car. Low–hanging mist shrouded the tops of the ridges and was making its way down.

'We need to get back before the weather gets any worse,' he said. 'Do you think you could put a spurt on?'

'Yes, you lead. I'll keep up.'

I felt that I had the energy to do it, and there was something exhilarating about trying to beat the storm.

'Put your hood up,' he told me. 'The air's going to feel like ice. The mist brings its own dangers with it. Stay close.'

I fussed with my clothing, and Fintry helped zip my hood, tucked my hair back from my face and pulled up the collar of my jacket. 'Snug as a bug.'

I smiled up at him, and then off we went at a fair pace.

We reached the car and he helped me off with my rucksack. He'd offered to carry it for me, but I'd insisted I could manage. A warm bath would soothe any aches later on. Besides, all the gardening work kept me fit.

He started up the engine. 'Unfortunately, the picnic is going to be put on hold. I have to get us out of here while there's still visibility on the roads.'

'We can have the picnic when we get home.'

He looked over at me as he put the car into reverse to turn it around. Were we thinking the same thing? *When we get home* sounded as if we were a couple.

I reached over the back seat to grab my camera from my rucksack to snap photos of the misty atmosphere. I also grabbed my small sketchpad to make notes of the colours I thought would capture the essence of the scenery. As I opened the sketchpad, a couple of little floral watercolours I'd done fell out. I went to tuck them back, but Fintry commented on one of them — distinctive blue flowers I'd painted weeks ago.

'Love–in–a–mist? Very appropriate for our first date.'

'First date?'

'Unless you don't want to mix business with pleasure.'

'No, I'm...I'm all for mixing pleasure with business,' I inadvertently said.

He grinned. 'I like a woman who gets her priorities right.'

I laughed and blushed.

'Rage or embarrassment? I hope it's the latter. I wouldn't want you to be angry with me, though we seem to be a couple who do things backwards.'

'Backwards? What do you mean?'

'Couples get together, there's a first date, usually dinner, and then at some point later on in their relationship they see each other naked. We've more or less done the naked thing.'

I started to laugh.

'And by the looks of this weather, we'll have the picnic when we get back to the house, which is surely backwards.'

'It is, but a picnic by the fireside is something to look forward to.'

'I like the sound of that,' he said.

By the time we got back to the house a thunder storm was brewing. Dark clouds tore across the sky. We hurried inside. Fintry lit the fire and I started to make dinner, leaving the picnic for later. He came through to help me. My ex never helped cook anything with me, and it was a novelty to have the company of a man who was happy to peel the potatoes and prepare the fish. By prepare I mean that he put pieces of breaded fish in the oven to bake while the potatoes boiled. I chopped spring onions to sprinkle over the potatoes after they'd been mashed. We worked well together. Even Snowdrop was pleased to join in, meowing when he smelled the fish cooking.

Fintry cut slices of iced fruit cake for after the main course. The cherries in the cake had been soaked in brandy and added to the flavour.

Taking our lead from the cat who flopped out in his bed after his dinner, we relaxed in front of the fire while the storm raged outside.

Fintry came over and sat beside me. He put his arms around me and we snuggled, just snuggled, watching the flames flicker in the hearth.

'It's been an adventurous day,' I said.

'Technically, it's not over. It's not midnight yet.' He leaned in and kissed me, passionately. I returned his passion, forgetting about everything except being with him.

'I've wanted to do that since I first saw you, Mairead. I hope you feel the same way about me.'

Did I ever.

He wrapped his arms around me, making me feel safe, wanted, desired, but then his phone rang.

'I don't want to answer it,' he said huskily.

I had a feeling he should. 'It could be important.'

He took the call. I saw his expression harden. 'Okay, I'm on my way.'

'What's wrong?'

He stood up. 'That was the harbour master. He says my yacht's in danger of breaking adrift. The storm's causing havoc with several of the boats. I have to go and secure it or move it further up the coast to a safer bay. That's his advice. I probably won't be back until the morning.'

'Do you want me to go with you? To help?' I offered.

'No, get some rest. I'll phone to let you know I'm okay.'

He grabbed his things and hurried out into the rain storm.

I went back and sat by the fire.

I fell asleep on the sofa. Fintry's call woke me up in the middle of the night. He assured me he was fine but was staying overnight at a hotel near the bay. The storm was causing further damage to boats all along the coast. The forecast said the storm would drift out to sea by the following day. 'I just don't want it taking my yacht with it,' he said.

'Take care. I'll see you when you get back.'

I went to bed and had another restless night.

CHAPTER NINE

Heliotrope

Rain belted down outside the kitchen window as I ate breakfast. A text message from Fintry assured me his yacht was okay and that he'd be back by the afternoon. That left little time for any further flower hunting. I was due to head back to the cottage in the evening.

I gazed out at the downpour. It wouldn't have been a day for trekking out in the hills anyway.

I used the time to pack my things and work on my watercolours. I added depth and details to the painting that included Fintry in the scene. The rough sketch was now a finished piece of art, a slice of life, of my time with the flower hunter. I couldn't shake off the feeling that something had changed between us, as if we weren't going to get a proper chance to fall in love. Silly thoughts, I supposed, but they hung in the air all that day, and I was thankful I had my colourful floral artwork to brighten the hours as I waited for him. Snowdrop had the right idea and snoozed in his basket most of the time.

Fintry arrived back in the early evening. I saw the headlights of his car sweep across the driveway of the farmhouse. I'd prepared a casserole for dinner and it was the first thing he remarked on when he came in and hung his jacket up.

'Dinner smells tasty. I'm starving. Nothing went according to plan, but the yacht's harboured safely. Sorry you've had a wasted trip. I wouldn't have invited you if I thought the weather was going to be so stormy.'

'We can't fight the elements.'

He gazed at me. 'I did try.'

I believed him.

He helped me serve up dinner and as we sat down I knew he had something to tell me, something he didn't want to say.

Although we were both hungry, neither of us made a start on the meal. He sighed and looked across the table at me.

'Say it. Whatever it is,' I told him.

'I have to go to London on business. It's where I planned to be before I heard there could be a new flower in this area. I was booked to give lectures and make a couple of appearances at events. Then I was going to sail to Europe. That's why the cottage was being leased out for a year.'

I listened, while he continued.

'I cancelled the tour dates, but because of the nature of my work, the organisers always allow for flexibility. If a flower hunter cancels a talk, for example, and then their search or work amounts to nothing more than a wild goose chase, the organisers are happy to reinstate the date.'

'So you're going to do what you originally planned because there's little chance of you finding a new flower in the Highlands?'

'Yes, and I've also had a couple of phone calls from organisers asking if I'm available because others have had to cancel and their schedules are looking pretty sparse. I've been asked to help fill the gaps if I'm available. It's important work. Important to a lot of people who rely on botanical expertise.'

'You should go then.'

He searched my face for any hint of a lie, but I meant what I said. That was the whole point of the cottage lease, to allow Fintry to go off on his business knowing the cottage was being looked after while he was away. Things needed to go back to how they were supposed to be.

'I'll be away for months,' he said. 'I'd like to keep in touch with you.'

I shook my head. 'I'd rather you didn't. I don't want to live like that. I've come out the other end of a toxic relationship that never felt settled and I really don't want to go there again. I'm not saying we won't ever see each other again, but I want to be free, to be me. I don't want to be waiting for something that may or may not work out.' My ex had drained me of all notion of hanging around waiting for love. And then there was Ethel's experience with a previous flower hunter who barely gave her the time of day after she'd waited for him. No, I refused to do this.

He nodded and I sensed the resignation in him. 'I appreciate you being straightforward, Mairead. And you're right. The life I live right now isn't one I would ask any woman to share with me.' He leaned forward, trying to make me understand. 'I live an adventurous life but a lonely one. I've reached a point where I yearn to settle down.' He ran a hand through the front of his hair. 'Okay, so I'd probably be off travelling sometimes, but not often. Not often at all. And I'd hope that the woman I'd marry would come with me.'

Marry? It wasn't a proposal, but it was a hint.

I remembered Tavion's message for me from the dressmaker about the bridal fabric she'd given me. '*She said you'd know what to do with it when the time came.*'

Would I? I only knew I'd never use Fintry's mother's bridal dress fabric to make a wedding gown. The marriage had ended in failure and sadness. No, I'd never use it for a wedding dress.

The atmosphere was heavy, so I tried to lighten the conversation. 'You'll be able to pop into the publishing offices and see Franklin when you're in London.'

The thought didn't seem to have occurred to him. 'Yes, I'll contact Franklin when I'm down.'

We ate dinner and didn't dwell on being apart. When it was time to leave, Fintry put my bags in my car. I cast a glance at the farmhouse as I drove off, sensing I'd never be back.

I followed Fintry in his car to where we'd arranged to meet that first night.

He parked his car and came over to talk to me through the driver's side window of my car. I kept the engine running. I didn't want any long goodbyes.

'I'm not going to say goodbye, Mairead. I've every intention of seeing you again someday.'

'Good luck with your trip to London and then Europe.' I'd no idea where he intended going. I didn't want to ask. I didn't want to know. I just wanted to drive off back to the cottage and gather my scattered senses.

'Are you sure you know the directions from here?' he said.

'Yes, I can find my own way back.'

He tapped the roof of the car and off I went, forcing myself not to be upset.

When I got back to the cottage I sighed with relief. Even though it was Fintry's house, it felt like home to me — welcoming and comforting. As there was next to nothing in the cottage of a personal nature that he'd left behind, it didn't remind me of him. It felt as it had before — a cosy cottage where I could relax and do what I wanted.

I made a mug of hot cocoa, lit the fire in the bedroom, put on the pyjamas I'd left behind and went to bed. I sat there, feeling the tension in my body ease as the heat from the fire and comforting bed made me relax.

'How was the art convention?' Tavion called to me as I walked down to the shops in the morning for fresh milk and bread.

'I had an adventurous time, thanks.'

'Get any painting done?'

'I did as a matter of fact.'

'Worth the trip then.'

I smiled at him. Had it been worth it?

'Ethel says to let her know when you get back. She was worried about you in the stormy weather.'

'I'll pop round to see her.'

'Be prepared to be quizzed on any scandalous things you got up to.'

'I didn't get up to anything like that.' Well, except for diving naked on Fintry and I certainly couldn't tell her that.

After buying my groceries I dropped them off at the cottage and then went to see Ethel. She was pleased to see me.

'Did you have a nice time?'

'It was interesting, but I'm glad to be back.'

We sat down at the fireside to chat. She eyed me carefully. 'Were you up to something? You've got a look about you like you've been romanced.'

I guffawed.

'Did you meet someone? Were you chatted up by a tall, handsome stranger?'

He was tall, handsome and not a stranger. I felt a blush, or perhaps it was guilt, burn across my cheeks.

Ethel giggled. 'Oh! You did get up to something. Was he lovely?'

I hated deceiving her. I was also worried. Ethel had an uncanny knack for seeing right through me.

'We had dinner and chatted about...things. About my art.'

Ethel sounded excited. 'Are you seeing him again?'

'Noooo. We didn't get up to anything, if you know what I mean.'

'Just flirting?'

I smiled. It was the nearest to the truth. White lies bordering on grey perhaps, but I couldn't tell her I'd met Fintry when I'd promised I'd keep his business private.

'Are you going to the party tonight?' she said.

'What party?'

'At the postmaster's house.'

'What's the party for?'

She shrugged. 'Nothing. Just a wee get together at his house. Everyone's welcome. You should go and kick up your heels.'

'There's dancing?'

'There's always dancing at his parties. Have you got a dress? Not that you have to wear anything special. Trousers and a top would do. It's only for a few of the locals. The postmaster's house has a long lounge that's ideal for jigging. It's just a bit of fun.'

'Actually, Ethel, I could do with that. So, yes. I'll go.'

'Great. I'll come by your cottage at seven–thirty and we'll walk across together.'

I knew most of the people at the party. The atmosphere and music was lively when we arrived. Ethel had her makeup on and underneath her warm coat she wore a dark sapphire velvet dress and her silvery blonde hair had been set in rollers.

The postmaster was over like a shot when he saw us, welcoming us in. He kept smiling at Ethel.

'Help yourself to the buffet ladies — and the punch. It's a potent brew I mixed myself to get the party going.'

Couples were whirling around the floor to céilidh music.

My black pumps had been the right choice to wear with my plaid skirt and red silk top. The heat from a large log fire made the room toasty and no doubt I'd be dancing soon. It was strange the effect this community had on me. I wasn't much of a dancer in the city. At dinner dances I tended to feel self–conscious, but here I felt as if no one would stare at me if I didn't get the steps right. No one was out to judge me, or snort disapproval down their snooty noses, like my ex's business colleagues, when my artistic flair didn't meet with their standards.

While the postmaster wasted no time getting Ethel on to the dance floor, I pondered having a glass of the so–called potent punch.

Slices of orange floated on the surface, giving the impression it was an innocuous fruity concoction. One sip told me otherwise.

'That'll put hair on your chest,' a man said to me, helping himself to a glass of it.

I didn't doubt it for a second.

I found myself looking around for Tavion and being disappointed when he wasn't there. I was sure he'd be at the party. Maybe he was busy.

After a particularly lively dance, the postmaster turned the music down to a peep. 'While you're all here, can I have your attention for a moment to remind you of the contributions needed for the forthcoming exhibition.'

Ethel, Hilda and other ladies I knew were nearby.

'There's a big, important exhibition coming up soon,' Ethel explained to me. 'The organisers have asked us to contribute any yarn, fabrics and textiles that are produced locally, by local people, to show the heritage of the things we make. The islanders are also taking part. Lots of different textiles, made by looms, or hand–printed fabrics, will be put on show in the city and then go on tour. I'm giving samples of my top yarns.'

'I've already handed in quilting fabrics,' said Hilda.

Ethel looked at me. 'What about your beautiful landscape art quilt? We need things that show the diversity and quality of what we make.'

Before I could reply, Hilda shook her head. 'Mairead's not eligible. She's not a local crafter.'

I had to agree, but then I remembered about the fabric in the wardrobe. One fabric in particular. 'What will happen to the items contributed?'

'They'll be well looked after,' the postmaster said, overhearing us discuss this. 'But the tour is a substantial one. If you have anything suitable, you'd have to be prepared for it being away for as long as two years before you got it back.'

'Do you have something?' Ethel asked me.

'I think I do. I have a large piece of vintage bridal fabric that was made locally.'

'Really? What is it?' said Hilda.

'It was Fintry's mother's wedding dress. The dressmaker gave it to me.'

The postmaster was the first to show his enthusiasm. 'That would be brilliant. We'd include her name and details. All items have to include those.'

'I'll hand it in to you tomorrow,' I told the postmaster.

He thanked me and turned up the music again and the dancing continued.

'I liked Fintry's mother,' said Ethel. 'She wanted to be part of the community here, and she was for a few years until the marriage split.'

'The dressmaker said I'd know what to do with the fabric when the time came,' I said.

Ethel nodded. 'I think Fintry's mother would appreciate not being forgotten.'

The remainder of the evening was a bundle of laughs and wild Scottish reels. In the midst of the dancing I wondered if Tavion would show up, but he never did.

Some of the other guests walked Ethel home. I walked back to the cottage after waving to them. There had been hugs all round at the end of a great night. A simple enough party, for no specific reason other than a local get together. I liked that.

The following afternoon I walked down to the post office and handed in the bridal fabric to the postmaster.

'Thank you, Mairead. I was asking around this morning, and a couple of people told me that this fabric was made for Fintry's mother by the dressmaker. So it really is quite special. I'll explain its importance to the exhibition organisers. I'm sure this will have pride of place. Vintage fabric of this quality is a rarity, so thanks again.'

I left the post office feeling I'd done the right thing. And there on the sea wall was Thimble, watching me. I blinked and he'd gone again.

I met Tavion on my way back to the cottage. I smiled at him. 'I thought you'd have been at the party last night. You missed a wild night.'

He had a guilty look on his face as if he hadn't missed a wild night at all. 'I had a dinner date in the city.'

I don't know why but this really took me aback. It shouldn't have, but I was sort of surprised. I guess I only thought of Tavion as the man on his own growing flowers and always willing to give me a helping hand.

I wasn't sure what to say. I smiled anyway.

'I have a friend, a woman I meet up with whenever she's in the city,' he explained. 'We've been friends for years.'

Friends with benefits judging by his expression.

'Well, I eh...I hope you had a wild time. A good time,' I corrected myself. 'A pleasant time.'

Shut up, I told myself. Shut up.

'I did. We did.' He sounded awkward.

I waved cheerily and hurried on.

As I arrived at the cottage I got a call from Franklin.

'I have a floral book cover that requires an illustration of heliotrope. Can you save the day? Can I have a high resolution copy of your heliotrope flowers? Need it asap. We're going to press soon.'

'I'll do that right now and email you,' I said.

I emailed a few minutes later after adjusting the copy.

I've attached a high res image of the heliotrope artwork. Hope this is suitable.

I read his response.

Perfect, Mairead. You'll be paid and credited as per usual. PS — I'm having a meeting in London next week with Fintry about his book. Will keep you posted re any artwork needed for his project.

I closed the laptop and felt a pang of longing. Fintry really had gone to London. I knew he was going, but there was still a little spark of hope that maybe, just maybe, he'd change his mind and decide to stay in Scotland. Ah well.

March was a great month for gardening. Spring flowers thrived in the cottage garden, bringing with them a sense of renewal. When I first started work in the garden in January, the ground had been left to overwinter. Now I prepared the topsoil to a fine tilth ready for sowing. Some seeds were potted and kept in the greenhouse or coldframes, depending on their needs.

Although the drainage in the garden was excellent, I took advantage of a dry spell to sow the mesembryanthemum seeds around the trellis archway. When they bloomed in summer they'd create a magic carpet of pink, purple, red and gold flowers. According to the notes in the garden folders, the archway was a sunny spot where the blue lobelia, climbing roses and sweet peas flourished. In the evenings the night scented stock filled the air with its wonderful fragrance around the arch. This led to an area of the garden that had a camomile lawn edged with taller plants such as the delphiniums, hollyhocks and chocolate coloured cornflowers. Further along, near a rockery, grew astilbe and the hardy pomegranate shrubs that the notes assured me didn't need fussing with. I couldn't wait for all of these beauties to flourish.

I had several varieties of sweet peas to sow in March and April including some of my favourites — Painted Lady, an old–fashioned sweet pea, and Perfume Delight.

After the March equinox, the daylight hours lengthened and I spent a lot of my time outdoors, pruning, clipping, planting and getting the garden in shape for summer.

It wasn't just the garden that shaped up. Although I was still on the slim side, I'd definitely toned up. And I had more energy, despite getting up early and working long hours. I'd yet to brave the cold sea, but I'd heard that the weather in April was often quite mild and a dip in the sea was recommended. I did enjoy walking along the shore, especially in the mornings.

I often waved to Tavion, and although he was always willing to help with any heavy lifting work in the garden, such as the time I needed a hand to sort the slabs that had become displaced near the shed, our relationship was no more than casual friendship. He was busy with his business, working in his fields. He invited me up one day to walk through a field of spring flowers before they were cut and ready for sale. I came home with an armful of them and put them in vases. The fragrance lasted for days in the cottage.

Apart from that, I felt as if we'd drifted, never quite the same as we'd been before I'd become close to Fintry and found out about Tavion's girlfriend in the city. Neither of us mentioned it, and this in itself created a gap we never managed to bridge. The sense of closeness had gone and I didn't believe it would ever come back.

The newspapers carried a story about the exhibition, and Fintry's mother's fabric was featured. I kept a clipping and put it in one of the flower hunter folders.

CHAPTER TEN

Night Scented Stock

Quilting kept me busy most evenings. Apart from being relaxing, it was part of my work. I fashioned all sorts of quilting projects, from throws, cushions and artwork quilts to a patchwork table runner, mug mat and sewing bag. I tried out the designs I'd created for blocks and motifs, adjusting and improving them.

Most of the blocks and motifs had floral designs that could be used by quilters and crafters. The motifs could be sewn as appliqué or made as complete blocks as part of a traditional quilt. They were also suitable for embroidery projects or coloured in and framed as paintings.

On one mild evening the warmth of the April sun lingered after dinner and I sat outside the front door of the cottage. The fragrance of the night scented stock flowers mixed with the scent of the sea was so calming. I stitched a small quilt project, sewing metallic gold thread along the edges of a flower pattern. The thread glistened like the surface light shining off the sea. A perfect evening when I realised I'd achieved what I'd originally set out to do — to find time to live and breathe without constant pressure, to leave the city behind and finish my book. And it was almost finished now. Franklin was delighted with the artwork and illustrations, the quilting designs and the elements I'd added due to being at the cottage. Elements that gave a quintessential feeling of bygone times when the quality of life was measured in special moments. Moments like this evening.

Sometimes I'd think about Fintry, especially when Franklin asked for a specific botanical illustration for Fintry's book. It was going to work out that our books would be published within weeks of each other. Franklin planned to double up on the marketing, linking me to both books to help with the launch of them.

And sometimes my heart would leap when I saw a blue and white yacht anchored at the harbour, mistakenly thinking he'd come home. These were thoughts I quickly quashed. Thoughts I didn't dare entertain. I bolstered myself with hopes that the man for me might be in London. Not Fintry, but someone else I'd never met. I'd thought about Franklin's offer and had decided I would go and work in London after the lease was finished. Daisy had worked there for years painting floral artwork for Franklin's company, and now lived in Cornwall. London didn't have to be forever.

The warm weather at the beginning of May gave me no excuse to avoid going for a swim in the sea.

Ethel gave me loads of encouragement. 'I'll paddle at the edges and keep an eye on you while you go for a dip.'

It was a particularly bright, sunny morning. I'd met Ethel at the wee shops and she suggested we didn't let it go to waste. She'd been extra busy with her classes throughout April and now that May had arrived she was due to be even busier. We tried to snap up any chance to have a chat, and she had asked me to teach quilting at the classes once a fortnight and I'd promised to do that.

She sat on the sea wall while I ran up to my cottage for a couple of towels.

'Don't run, Mairead. There's no hurry. I'll wait.'

I ran anyway. She didn't know I wanted to make a quick flask of tea and cut slices of the chocolate cake I'd baked for a makeshift picnic.

I rustled everything together, stuffed it into one of my quilted craft bags, and ran back down with my hair up in a high ponytail. Ethel sat with her eyes closed, enjoying the warmth of the sun on her face.

'Here we are,' I said, hooking the bag on to my shoulder. 'A dip and then a cuppa.'

She grinned at me. 'Perfect. Let's go.'

We walked down the steps to the sandy shore. The air felt warm, and we were shielded from the wind by the cliffs. It felt as if the sun beamed down on this part of the coast and the thought of swimming in the sea was less daunting.

Ethel settled down on what she called 'a comfy rock.' I insisted she sit on the towels to cushion her backside. She kicked her shoes off. 'The sand feels moderately warm on the soles of my feet.'

Another sign that the sea water wouldn't be freezing cold. I hoped.

I took my clothes off to reveal the turquoise blue swimsuit I'd thrown on while the kettle boiled. It was the only one I owned and had seen very little use in its entire life.

'Oh, if Fintry could see you now, his heart would flip.'

She'd continued to bring Fintry's name up in our conversations, and I always felt awkward that she didn't know what had happened between us.

I looked along the coast. 'We're the only ones here. No one else is thinking of going in for a swim.'

'Ach, they're all chickens. In you go, Mairead. You test the water. Depending on how loud you scream, I'll think about having a paddle.'

I grinned at her. 'Cheers, Ethel.'

The sun felt warm and I loved the sense of freedom, wearing only my swimming costume, feeling the sand on my feet. I squinted against the dazzling light glistening off the surface of the sea. The water was clear. I could see right down to the sand and shiny pebbles.

'Okay,' I said. 'Here goes.' I dipped one foot tentatively into the water and let out an exaggerated yell, causing Ethel to gasp and then giggle, realising I was winding her up.

'Wee rascal,' she muttered.

I waded into the water. It was cold but pleasantly so. Refreshing.

'How is it?'

'Invigorating.' I waded deeper until it was up to my waist. 'I'm going in,' I called to her and dived below the surface, emerging spluttering and laughing.

Ethel got up and paddled at the edge. 'It's not bad for May.'

I swam a short distance along the coast, turned and swam back again.

Ethel waved to me. 'This is the life, eh, Mairead?'

Indeed it was.

I emerged reluctantly from the water and wrapped a towel around me.

Ethel had let her feet dry naturally in the sun and sat on the towel I'd given her. 'Will I pour us a cuppa?' She held up the flask and balanced the cups on the rock.

'Yes, thanks.' I kept the towel on and squeezed the water out of the ends of my ponytail, letting my hair drip on my shoulders. 'It's beautiful here. No wonder you've never wanted to leave.'

'Have you any plans for the future? You mentioned you were offered work at the publishers in London.'

'I think I'll accept the offer, but I'll miss all of this.'

'Remember I mentioned that a cottage near here was going to be up for grabs?'

I nodded.

'Well, someone's grabbed it.' Ethel sounded disappointed. 'Apparently it's a young woman who is into sewing.'

I tried not to sound envious. 'Never mind. I couldn't have considered taking on a second lease.' My finances had picked up recently. I'd noticed I had more money in my account than I'd estimated. I hadn't studied it in detail and figured it was the payments from Franklin that had given it a boost. 'I doubt the owner would've waited until I was ready to lease it. They wouldn't have wanted it to lie empty for months.'

'True enough,' said Ethel. 'There's always demand for property in this area. Nothing is on the market for long.'

I recalled how excited I'd felt when I saw the flower hunter's cottage advertised, and then managed to secure the lease. And suddenly, my heart sank, thinking of how things had started out. And then thinking about Fintry.

I gave Ethel a slice of chocolate cake wrapped in a napkin. 'Totally impractical for eating down the shore.'

'When did chocolate cake ever have to be practical?' she said, happy to accept it.

We sat quiet for a moment, and I tried to brush thoughts of Fintry aside.

'I thought I saw Fintry's yacht in the harbour the other day, but it wasn't him,' she said.

'I thought the same.' I knew I sounded melancholy.

'What is it? What's wrong, Mairead?'

I sighed heavily, shook my head, gazing out at the sparkling sea.

'Is it secrets?'

Ethel was a perceptive one. I nodded.

'Someone else's secrets?'

I nodded again.

'Don't fuss yourself over that,' she insisted. 'Keeping other folks secrets is messy, but it doesn't change anything between you and me. I understand. I'm sure if it was up to you, you'd confide in me.'

'I would, Ethel.'

'And that's okay.'

'What's going on here?'

We turned to see Tavion striding towards us.

'Chocolate cake and chatter,' Ethel told him.

'Is there room for one more?' he asked.

'Girl talk,' Ethel emphasised.

Tavion put his hands up in an exaggerated gesture and started to walk off. 'I'll be on my way, girls.'

We let him go without another word.

Ethel glanced at me. 'It's not Tavion then, is it?'

She could tell from my casual reaction to him. 'No.'

'I won't pry any further.'

She was quiet for a moment and then said, 'I've got some gossip that might interest you. The postmaster is responsible for mail all along this coast. When folk go on holiday, they can ask for their letters to be kept at his PO boxes. Anyway, there were people who came back from holiday and when they picked up their mail from him they let slip that Fintry had been staying in their farmhouse after he left his cottage.'

'Really?'

'Yes, he was there round about the time you were at that art convention.'

I smiled tightly.

'Fintry's been abroad for months now from what I hear. But it just goes to show that when we all thought he was away, he was actually just up the coast in his friends' farmhouse.'

'That is interesting.'

'It is, isn't it?' She looked at me and then we both smiled at each other.

The sun continued to shine brightly.

'There's a fair heat in the sun today. Do you fancy having another swim?'

I did. I stood up and shrugged my towel off. 'I certainly do.'

'I'm going to be daring,' she said. 'I'm going for another paddle and this time I'm wading in until it's up to my knees.'

We laughed and enjoyed another dip.

I swam up and down while Ethel tried not to get her dress wet. She bunched up the hem, revealing a lovely pair of thighs, and waded into the sea.

From far up on the harbour's edge a cheeky whistle sounded from the lips of the postmaster.

'You behave yourself,' Ethel shouted to him and then continued to splash around in the water.

I was practically living in the garden. The weather in May continued to be brilliant. Bright blue skies, mild sea breezes, and the occasional rain storm, mainly during the night, created a freshly washed landscape in the mornings.

I ate breakfast outside on the patio surrounded by flowers and trees. On the occasional overcast morning I'd sit inside the shed with the door open enjoying the scent of the freesia growing nearby along with the gypsophila, and lily of the valley — little bell–shaped flowers that always made me think of weddings.

A niche of the garden had every hue of blue you could wish for. From the pale blue forget–me–nots, cornflowers and traditional bluebells to the vibrant sea holly and love–in–a–mist, the blues always made me want to paint them.

Near the strawberry patch were, appropriately, the gomphrena 'strawberry fields' flowers. The strawberries hadn't reached fruition, but the bright red flowers were well ahead.

After breakfast I'd work in the garden, stopping only to prepare lunch. Afternoons were when I mowed the lawn, nurtured the roses and any other flowers vying for attention.

I'd become quite partial to having tea and scones with jam and cream in the afternoons, sitting at the wooden table in the arbour under a garden umbrella. Here, I'd sketch and paint. Depending on the glare, it was usually easier to paint shaded from the direct sunlight, especially when working with watercolours. This was the time I left every electronic device inside the cottage. No laptop, no mobile phone. No interruptions, emails or text messages. Not for these little pockets when I could imagine that this is what life used to be like way back when the cottage was first built. Little had changed. The garden was recognisable from the old photographs and the view was the same as it had been for decades.

One afternoon at the end of May that's what I was doing when I felt someone watching me. A sense, a shiver, a knowing I was being watched. I glanced up from my artwork and looked around the garden. Nothing.

I continued painting delicate pink fairy lantern flowers and beautiful blue viper's bugloss. And all the while I wondered if these lovely flowers would transfer well into quilt block designs.

'Hello, Mairead,' a voice said.

I looked up and there was Fintry. I blinked, thinking at first it was my imagination, but no, it was him.

'Fintry,' I gasped. My heart jolted when I saw him. He wore dark tan trousers and a light cream shirt open at the neck. He looked fit and strong — and seriously handsome.

He walked across the lawn towards me, dipping his head beneath the rose entwined archway. The roses had a mind of their own and despite trimming them, they'd claimed the top of the archway. I had no problem walking under it, but Fintry's six foot plus stature was too tall and he had bend to walk under it.

'I tried to phone you, but you didn't pick up,' he said. 'I also emailed a couple of hours ago. You didn't reply.'

'When I'm out here I often leave the phone and laptop inside. I switch off when I'm in the garden.'

He nodded. 'I used to do the same.'

'Did you?'

'Yes. It was nice to enjoy the peace and quiet, like my grandparents had in the past.'

He walked nearer and stopped at the edge of the lawn.

Oh how I ached when I looked at him. But I couldn't let him see how he affected me, not for a second.

'I shouldn't actually be here,' he admitted.

'No?'

'No. I should be halfway to the Azores by now after Cannes.'

'I think you may have taken a wrong turn.' I tried to sound light–hearted when in fact my heart was thundering in my chest.

He shook his head. 'No, I took the wrong turn earlier this year.' He walked closer. 'I'm eh...hoping that it's not too late to turn back. To get on the right path.'

'A detour?'

'A complete turnaround, with a sincere apology for making the stupidest mistake of my life.'

He was beside me now, gazing down at me as I sat at the table.

'Is it too late, Mairead? Am I too late?'

I knew what he meant.

'The thing is,' I began, 'I'm obliged to look after this garden. It belongs to a flower hunter. I promised I'd take care of it while he was away.'

His sensual lips curved, suppressing a smile. 'A promise is a promise.'

I nodded firmly.

'What about a compromise?' he suggested.

'What did you have in mind?'

'I could help you look after the cottage, for summer, the autumn, the winter...the foreseeable future in fact. What do you think?'

I took a steadying breath. 'I quite like that idea.'

His eyes sparkled with mischief. 'Quite like?'

'It's the money issue,' I explained. 'Every time I try to pay my monthly lease, the payment is refused. And the initial down payment was returned too. My bank account is looking a lot healthier these days.'

'Maybe the flower hunter doesn't want to accept any payment from you and has repaid the money back to you.'

'It appears that way. Of course I'm wondering why?'

'I could be completely wrong, but perhaps he's trying make amends for being a fool to risk losing the only woman he can't stop thinking about. The only woman who has ever made him want to change his lifestyle and live a settled, but prosperous, life with her.'

'I'd love to believe that.'

He took my hands in his and pulled me close to him, so close I could hear the strength of his heart. It didn't falter. It didn't seem to lie. It didn't sound like the false promises I'd had from men in the past. It sounded true.

'You can believe it, Mairead.' He leaned down and kissed me, making me forget everything except the two of us. When the world stopped being busy, when all was settled and quiet, that's all that really mattered. Fintry and me.

We spent the summer together at the cottage, and planned to continue this into the autumn and winter. When Fintry had to go to London to discuss further details about his book with Franklin, and attend a couple of business meetings, he took me with him. On his yacht. We sailed down together.

Franklin couldn't be happier for us, neither could my grandparents or Ethel. I'm not so sure about Tavion. That rivalry between them still runs deep.

Fintry has hinted that he's going to propose to me, so I'll receive that marriage proposal after all.

And I received a pre–emptive message from the dressmaker, wishing us a happy life together. She sent a parcel for me too. It contained several metres of pure oyster coloured silk edged with hand sewn flowers in metallic silver and gold threads. Sewn by the dressmaker herself.

I was sure there was magic sewn into the fabric. Perhaps not magic as we know it, but magic of the heart. A belief that people can care about each other, about those in their communities, even from afar.

She wrote in her message that I would know what to do with the fabric when the time came.

And I did.

I would use it to make my wedding dress when I married Fintry.

End

Now that you've read the story, you can try your hand at making some of the sewing, knitting and papercraft projects available from the book's accompanying website.
Here is the link: http://www.de-annblack.com/flower

De-ann has been writing, sewing, knitting, quilting, gardening and creating art and designs since she was a little girl. Writing, dressmaking, knitting, quilting, embroidery, gardening, baking cakes and art and design have always been part of her world.

About the Author:

Follow De-ann on Instagram @deann.black

De-ann Black is a bestselling author, scriptwriter and former newspaper journalist. She has over 80 books published. Romance, crime thrillers, espionage novels, action adventure. And children's books (non-fiction rocket science books and children's fiction). She became an Amazon All-Star author in 2014 and 2015.

She previously worked as a full-time newspaper journalist for several years. She had her own weekly columns in the press. This included being a motoring correspondent where she got to test drive cars every week for the press for three years.

Before being asked to work for the press, De-ann worked in magazine editorial writing everything from fashion features to social news. She was the marketing editor of a glossy magazine. She is also a professional artist and illustrator. Fabric design, dressmaking, sewing, knitting and fashion are part of her work.

Additionally, De-ann has always been interested in fitness, and was a fitness and bodybuilding champion, 100 metre runner and mountaineer. As a former N.A.B.B.A. Miss Scotland, she had a weekly fitness show on the radio that ran for over three years.

De-ann trained in Shukokai karate, boxing, kickboxing, Dayan Qigong and Jiu Jitsu. She is currently based in Scotland.

Her colouring books and embroidery design books are available in paperback. These include Floral Nature Embroidery Designs and Scottish Garden Embroidery Designs.

Also by De-ann Black (Romance, Action/Thrillers & Children's books). See her Amazon Author page or website for further details about her books, screenplays, illustrations, art and fabric designs.
www.De-annBlack.com

Romance books:

Sewing, Crafts & Quilting series:
1. The Sewing Bee
2. The Sewing Shop

Quilting Bee & Tea Shop series:
1. The Quilting Bee
2. The Tea Shop by the Sea

Heather Park: Regency Romance

Snow Bells Haven series:
1. Snow Bells Christmas
2. Snow Bells Wedding

Summer Sewing Bee
Christmas Cake Chateau

Cottages, Cakes & Crafts series:
1. The Flower Hunter's Cottage ✓
2. The Sewing Bee by the Sea
3. The Beemaster's Cottage
4. The Chocolatier's Cottage
5. The Bookshop by the Seaside

EMBROIDERY COTTAGE

Sewing, Knitting & Baking series:
1. The Tea Shop
2. The Sewing Bee & Afternoon Tea
3. The Christmas Knitting Bee
4. Champagne Chic Lemonade Money
5. The Vintage Sewing & Knitting Bee

The Tea Shop & Tearoom series:
1. The Christmas Tea Shop & Bakery
2. The Christmas Chocolatier
3. The Chocolate Cake Shop in New York at Christmas
4. The Bakery by the Seaside
5. Shed in the City

Tea Dress Shop series:
1. The Tea Dress Shop At Christmas
2. The Fairytale Tea Dress Shop In Edinburgh
3. The Vintage Tea Dress Shop In Summer

Christmas Romance series:
1. Christmas Romance in Paris.
2. Christmas Romance in Scotland.

Romance, Humour, Mischief series:
1. Oops! I'm the Paparazzi
2. Oops! I'm A Hollywood Agent
3. Oops! I'm A Secret Agent
4. Oops! I'm Up To Mischief

The Bitch-Proof Suit series:
1. The Bitch-Proof Suit
2. The Bitch-Proof Romance
3. The Bitch-Proof Bride

The Cure For Love
Dublin Girl
Why Are All The Good Guys Total Monsters?
I'm Holding Out For A Vampire Boyfriend

Action/Thriller books:
Love Him Forever
Someone Worse
Electric Shadows
The Strife Of Riley
Shadows Of Murder
Cast a Dark Shadow

Children's books:
Faeriefied
Secondhand Spooks
Poison-Wynd
Wormhole Wynd
Science Fashion
School For Aliens

Colouring books:
Flower Nature
Summer Garden
Spring Garden
Autumn Garden
Sea Dream
Festive Christmas
Christmas Garden
Christmas Theme
Flower Bee
Wild Garden
Faerie Garden Spring
Flower Hunter
Stargazer Space
Bee Garden
Scottish Garden Seasons

Embroidery Design books:
Floral Nature Embroidery Designs
Scottish Garden Embroidery Designs

Printed in Great Britain
by Amazon